How to Make Ghosts

by

Mistress Elena Hexthorn

About the Book

'How to Make Ghosts' is Miss Hexthorn's satirical erotic novel debut.

…Disillusioned by a dead-end relationship, pragmatic Isobel strikes a deal with a demon. The demon offers Isobel the chance to sell her boyfriend's body to him, in return for a better (kinky) life. But soon, she finds that the transaction proves to be more complicated than she was led to expect. Along the way, Isobel finds out many secrets about the inner workings of the underworld and engages in some extremely wild, kinky sex. Set against the backdrop of Hampstead Heath, London, U.K. "How to Make Ghosts" empowers all who read it to explore the boundaries of their own true, erotic wildness. This darkly satirical story will also take you inside the thoughts and fantasies of underworld entities. This book is also a recipe for some very kinky re-enactment scenarios.

About the Author

Elena Hexthorn has run dungeons and fetish clubs in London since the early 1990's, including the long-standing fetish event: London Fetish Fair. Hailing from Massachusetts, U.S.A, Ayrshire, Scotland, Surrey & London, Miss Hexthorn is a trained, skilled BDSM practitioner which has served to create accuracy within her writing. Elena Hexthorn writes extremely kinky fantasy and black comedy erotica novels that often divulge the desires of underworld creatures. With strong elements of the gothic lifestyle, her stories provide many BDSM scenes depicting such elements of realism that you will feel that you are in the story. When she is not writing, she is usually subjugating or tormenting a slave, getting tied to a tree in a forest for fun, going to concerts, working on her screenwriting, sewing, playing with her cats, or studying TV presenting & film production. For fun, Elena has a passion for film photography and painting in oils. These skills help to compliment the experience of her writing. She loves to interact with readers especially via social media.

How to Make Ghosts

Elena Hexthorn

© copyright 2017 Elena Hexthorn

The right of Elena Hexthorn to be identified as author of this work has been asserted in accordance with the Copyright, Designs and Patents Act 1988

All Rights Reserved

No reproduction, cope or transmission of the publication may be made without written permission. No paragraph of this publication may be reproduced, copied or transmitted save the written permission of the publisher, or in accordance with the provisions of the Copyright Act 1956 (as amended)

Any person who does any unauthorised act in relation to this publication may be liable to criminal prosecution and civil claims for damages.

This is a work of fiction. Names, characters, businesses, places, events and incidents are either the products of the author's imagination or used in a fictitious manner. Any resemblance to actual persons, living or dead, or actual events is purely coincidental.

This edition published 2017

Dedication

This book is dedicated to my 3 little Droogs: Mercury, Minerva & Jupiter.

May your respective 27 little lives be charmed ones.

Table of Contents

Chapter 1 The Heath 1

Chapter 2 The Walk 34

Chapter 3 The Deal 61

Chapter 4 Freedom 89

Chapter 5 The Black Dog 114

Chapter 6 The Rite 139

Chapter 7 The Knife 166

Chapter 8 Bubble's Pizza 190

Chapter 9 Mistress Isobel 220

Chapter 10 Parliament 241

Chapter 11 Ghost Maker 267

Chapter 1 The Heath

Isobel brushed through the chaos of her long red tresses. She smeared dark metallic green lip gloss across her lips with a degree of precision. She packed her handbag and looked across the scene in her living room. Her boyfriend Sam was sitting at her desk, staring. His eyes were transfixed on the computer whilst typing short chat messages in a forum. It was another typical Friday night. She knew instinctively what she had to look forward to. This night would be yet another evening of watching him drink vodka whilst chatting to his friends on the internet. It's what he did every single weekend. God, he was boring.

She dressed in a long dark green leather coat and grabbed a set of keys from a hook in the hallway. She stuffed the keys in her pocket. She sat down on a chaise longue in the living room and began to pull on her black leather ankle boots. Sam addressed her without looking up from his computer.

'Where are you going at this time-of-night?' he said.

'Well, for a start it's only 8 o'clock,' she replied defensively. 'I don't know if you have noticed, but it's November 5th. It's Guy Fawkes night. I am going up to the top of the heath to watch the fireworks.'

Isobel paused and waited for his reply. Different thoughts buzzed around inside her mind. It would have been nice if he had offered to go up the hill with her the way normal couples would. But, she resigned herself to the knowledge that he was basically a computer shut-in now. All the passion had died within the first 3 months of their relationship. Now, it was five years down the line in their relationship, and now they treated each other more like flatmates. The divisions between them had ballooned out of control. Isobel had always lived in a silent hope that things might turn around and improve. Every day she tried to give the failing circumstances another chance, but nothing ever seemed to get better.

'Ugh,' he sighed. 'The thought of all those shouty kids and chavs smoking skunkweed, setting off crappy fireworks. Going up to the top of the heath doesn't sound like fun at all.'

'No,' huffed Isobel. 'You're quite right. It sounds awful. I guess I should just stay here and watch you talk to people on the other side of the world whilst simultaneously ignoring me instead. That sounds much more festive.'

Isobel stamped her heel down into her boot to fit it in place. She got up and slammed the door as she left. As she walked through the passageways in her block of flats towards the exit. She felt a wave of deflation and isolation caused by yet another circular argument with

Sam. She crossed the road and headed towards the cloak of darkened streets that lay before her. Sometimes slipping into the darkness made her feel more comfortable. She liked how disappearing into the blackness had a way of ensuring that no one would find her. And if no one could find her, no one could say or do anything destructive to her. She always felt an immense feeling of liberation when she exercised her power to disappear. At first, the only sound she could hear were her own footsteps on the pavement. But as she got closer to the heath she started to see small groups of couples and sporadic gatherings of different families begin to meander their way up to the top of Parliament Hill. She could hear them chatting and laughing as they walked.

Feeling momentarily isolated, Isobel sighed to herself quietly.

She walked past a collection of tidy little gardens of the terraced houses and looked at the glow of each window as it casted shadows onto the plants and flowers. Soon, she found herself at the foot of the bridge that crossed over onto Hampstead Heath.

Isobel thought about Sam. She felt that it was a pity that he never wanted to leave the flat. He was a good looking, intelligent sort of guy. But, over time he had cloistered himself off and started living on the internet. It was a source of irritation for Isobel. When they had first gotten together he had been very open-minded. He was always up for going out or trying fun new things. Now, all he ever seemed to want to do was talk to strangers on the other side of the planet. She did love him. But there was nothing left she could do to reset their situation back to its original state. After many arguments with him, she resolved to give up on her efforts. She just carried on going out to places on her own. He didn't want to take advantage of the fact that London was on their doorstep, whereas she felt that she did.

Isobel decided to put those irritating thoughts to one side. After all, it was only going to spoil the fireworks. She decided it was just too much aggravation to bother to give any more attention to that line of thought. She carried on walking towards the summit.

She ascended the path, following behind the outlines other people in the shadows as they filed up the sparsely lit walkway to the top of Parliament Hill. She passed by several banks of huge oak trees. She loved visiting green spaces that were cloaked in darkness. As she approached the top of the clearing, she could see groups of people chatting, drinking and facing the twinkling lights of the city. Skyscrapers were blinking in the distance. This was accented by an occasionally passing aircraft that would pass over them. The panorama over London at night was a familiar view to her from this location. Isobel joined the throng of people, all patiently waiting for the fireworks over London to start. Groups of teenagers drank bottles of cheap fizzy pink wine. One or of the two sets of random, jumper- wearing couples drank champagne from glasses with wicker baskets planted by their feet. A swathe of local lads passed around half bottles of vodka to each other, which they drank straight from a neck. Every time that she had walked up the hill to see the fireworks, she experienced the same feeling. Everyone there seemed to have a way of sharing this day of the year on the Heath with an equal pleasure. But to her, it seemed like they all had a different polarity of view. There was never any acrimony at the site. The fireworks were always the primary focus of the evening for everyone present. She liked the strange anonymity of the event.

She smiled as she watched the parties of people. They loitered in small groups at different points across the field in the blackness. She noticed that several of the groups were trying to light the fuel attached to their Chinese sky lanterns. This was always a fun tradition to witness because it rarely went well. The fuel was notoriously hard to light. The act of trying to light the lanterns had to vie with the gusts of wind as it blasted across the heath. Invariably, when they did manage to light the fuel; it wouldn't be long before something would go horribly wrong. A general first reaction from a group would be something like a roar of excitement from each gathering of lantern lighters, followed by a cheer as the lantern ascended into the night sky. Frequently after that, a lantern would malfunction and opt to drag along the grass. The unpredictable direction of the sky lantern would usually ambush another group of people, who would then scatter as the flying ball of paper and fire hurtled towards their group. Isobel found it delightful to watch the carnage. She was thankful too, that there was somewhere left in London that wasn't at the cruel mercy of the health-and-safety jobsworth types. She loved the effects of unpredictable chaos sometimes. It made her feel free.

By 8:30 pm, everyone had chosen a spot to stand around the lower heath. Others stood at the top of the summit to watch the firework display begin to start. The sight over the London skyline could be a beautiful one. Twinkling lights from the skyscrapers near the Thames began to glisten with scintillating explosions in every colour of the spectrum. The heath crowd cheered along with every bellowing explosion as it filled the sky with beautiful light. Families with children lit Roman candles in small clusters against the black backdrop of the field. Isobel produced her camera and took a few sneaky shots of their faces against the phosphorescence. She enjoyed photographing the effect of unusual types of light. It would always produce something interesting. The illuminated expressions the people made as they gazed at roman candles were often filled with a kind of innocent wonder. Fireworks had a way of bringing out the youth in people. It was for this reason that she enjoyed fireworks events.

Isobel put her camera back in her bag and moved to light up a cigarette. She loved the sound of the haphazard whizzing of the fireworks as they exploded above the Thames river. To her surprise, someone lit her cigarette for her. She looked to the left. It was Sam. He was smiling. Isobel smiled back and kissed him.

'Thank you,' she said. 'I am so glad you changed your mind. There's more to life than just the inside of our flat, you know. I was hoping you would come out.'

'I know. From the moment that you walked out of the door, it took me 2 minutes to change my mind. I followed behind you and watched you walk up the heath. I admit I have been feeling a bit cooped up lately. Besides, this is the best time of year to come up here. The fireworks always look amazing against this blackness.'

Sam lit a cigarette for himself and drew the smoke in sharply. They stood and watched the fireworks until the last colourful incendiary device went spiralling into the air. It fizzled out with a lacklustre pop. The crowd cheered and clapped at the finish. Gradually, groups of people in twos and fours began to usher away from the top of the hill. Others stood chatting and drinking. Isobel turned to Sam.

'Well I guess it's time to go back then,' she said.

'Oh, I don't know about that,' he replied. It's remarkably mild for this time of the year. We may as well go for a little stroll on the heath.'

Sam produced a flask full of gin from his jacket.

'Where did you get that?' exclaimed Isobel.

'Just something I was saving for a special occasion,' he said warmly.

Isobel took a swig from the flask. 'Mm, Blueberry gin! I love it!'

'I know,' said Sam.

Sam took a drink from the flask. He took Isobel's hand and led her along one of the choice of dark, winding paths that led into the wooded part of the heath.

'I haven't got a light with me,' said Isobel.

'Don't worry,' he replied. 'We don't need a torch. Give yourself some time to adjust to the light. It won't seem so dark in a few minutes. There's a bright moon out tonight.'

Isobel took Sam's arm and felt a tiny glimmer of hope. She thought that perhaps things would start to get better for them both again.

'Okay, but for now- you lead the way. My eyes are still adjusting,' she replied. 'My feet are a still a little unsteady.'

The two ambled over a sculpted concrete bridge beside an overgrown, dark pond. Creatures rustled and croaked by the edges of the trees that framed the water. Isobel spied another couple as they stood on the bridge, kissing. Isobel wished that had been her and Sam, but those moments had long since been few and far between lately. However, Isobel still took some solace in the fact that at least Sam wanted to be outside. Even if he was still drinking, at least it was with her. And the gin *was* commendable. She could feel the warm glow of the blueberry gin start to relax her. It didn't really matter where they were going, she felt. She was happy because they were both outside and together. This was first day that had been a marked improvement after a slew of monotonous months.

They carried on walking until they reached a dirt path which was heavily lined with enormous trees. They could hear owls hooting and creatures scuttling about in the thicket. Shadows made by the waving branches danced along the ground in front of them as they walked. The path was very tumultuous. The roots of the trees had forced their way up onto ground level, making the path even harder to navigate in the dark. Isobel could feel herself losing her step from time to time, but would grab Sam's arm more tightly when she felt like she was going to trip.

'Oh!' said Isobel, nearly tripping. 'Hang on, give me a second. My eyes still need to adjust. Let me sit on this tree root for a few minutes.'

'It's okay,' replied Sam. 'We have arrived. This is the place I wanted to show you.'

'Oh really?' answered Isobel, with a supercilious tone. 'And just what exactly did you want to show me?'

Sam stood staring at her for a minute silently. At first, Isobel smiled. She looked up at him and wondered what must be going through his head that he needed to spend so much time staring at her. He had had several years to look at her, for so this strange act of his studying her made her feel a little bit exposed. Isobel also sensed that his staring was going on for a bit too long. She started to feel disconcerted. It made her think that perhaps he was either daydreaming, or drunk. Sam continued to stare, silently. It was as though he was in a trance. He stood rigidly. It made her feel distinctly uncomfortable. Isobel decided she had to do something to break the silence.

'What's wrong Sam?' she said softly.

He continued to stand stalk still, staring at her.

'Sam, what's up?' she said with a bit more concern.

Sam took one step towards where she was sitting on the tree root. Still, he gave no answer.

His eyes turned to look up to the top of the tree. Isobel followed the path of his gaze but she couldn't see very well in the darkness. Slowly, she watched as his eyes followed the length of the tree back to the roots on the earth floor. He again fixed his gaze on her.

He walked towards her and crouched down to face her on her own level.

'Do you love me?' he said queried.

'Yes,' replied Isobel. 'I keep trying to, when you let me.'

'Do you trust me?' he asked.

'Again, I keep trying to,' she said, with a matter-of-fact tone. 'When you aren't immersed in the internet. I am still here for you. I like when we are out. I want us to do more things together. I am glad you came outside tonight. Where are you going with this?'

He leaned over to her and kissed her deeply. He grabbed her throat and licked her neck. Isobel responded with a little surprise, but still enthusiastically. They embraced. Sam propped Isobel up against the tree. He grabbed Isobel, pulling her towards him forcefully. He ran his hands over the lines of her waist before moving his hands up to grab her breasts roughly. Isobel felt a surge of excitement. He pulled her breasts free from her black bra and began to suck on her nipples. She could feel the cool air making them hard. She looked down and felt his saliva was making her nipples shiny and wet. Sam forced his hands down her skirt and grabbed her pussy with more force. He had a way of being physically demanding that she always liked. But, it had been a long time since he had acted this way.

In the beginning of their relationship, he seemed to be horny with her all the time. It was exciting. He had a way of just taking what he wanted from her sexually without trying to negotiate some form of contract beforehand. Now, he suddenly started to act the way she had remembered him. He was acting the way he had, when they had first started dating. She loved his spontaneous lack of restraint. Neither was she particularly worried about being discovered. They were on the heath in the dark. She surmised that if anyone did spot them, they would probably take off once they had figured out what the two of them were up to.

Sam grabbed both of her wrists and pinned her up against the tree trunk. He unbuckled his belt, ripped through her black tights and swiftly forced his cock inside of her. She was dripping wet from the shock of this instantaneous action. Isobel moaned. Somehow his cock felt different from the last time they had had sex. Then again, she thought to herself, it had been so long since that had happened that maybe her pussy had tightened up. The thought passed in and out of her mind again like a flash.

Isobel gasped as he fucked her furiously against the tree trunk. He mauled at her breasts and ass wildly. He was more like a primal stranger than the Sam she had come to know. Momentarily, he stopped and forced her head down onto his cock.

'Spit on it,' he demanded. Isobel obliged.

She could feel his cock get harder as he forced her head onto his hard prick. He grabbed her by her hair and began the act of skull-fucking her. Isobel felt a slight wave of hysteria as she gasped for air between his thrusts into her mouth. She straightened her neck and made a concerted effort to comply with his desire. She enjoyed the intensity of it.

Sam groaned as she forced the cock into the back of her throat. Isobel choked. She spat up a small amount of fluid from her throat and wretched for a moment, before returning to the task of spiking her lips over the entire length of his cock. He pulled her head away and pushed her to down to the ground. Mercilessly, he ravaged her body against the tree roots of the earthen floor. For a fleeting moment, she puzzled about where this new energy was coming from in him. It felt so alien. She felt the roots of the trees digging against her back as he fucked her. Had she not been so distracted by this new turn of events, she may have taken more notice of their cold, dark surroundings. But the pleasure she felt by far outweighed any discomfort she might be experiencing, so she paid no attention to it.

Sam positioned Isobel onto all fours and plunged his cock into her pussy from behind. He grabbed her long hair and wrapped it around her neck.

'You are such a fucking dirty slut, aren't you?' he said with a cruel but playful tone to his voice.

'Yes,' she gasped.

'And you are going to cum for me aren't you, dirty slut,' he added.

'Yes, y..ess,' rasped Isobel.

Sam began to tighten his grip. She could feel herself being slowly starved of oxygen. Simultaneously one of the most enormous orgasms began to build inside of her. It was the most intoxicating mixture of panic superseded by a compelling force of impending ecstasy.

'I think someone's in the woods quietly watching us,' he taunted. 'If they get any closer you will end up being seen like this, on all fours getting fucked. So, you had better cum soon. Come before you run out of air, slut.'

Governing her strength, she thrusted back on his cock. She could feel a moment of agonising euphoria. She blacked out, seeing only tiny stars and blackness. Her mind lost all track of time and swam in a moment of pure unrefined, joy. It felt like an internal firework had been set off inside of her body. She tensed as the rising set of insanely delicious chemicals shot up into the back of her brain. She could feel her pussy flooding and gushing as she came. Now thrusting harder, she could feel Sam straining as he pushed his cock deep inside of her. Without a word, he rapidly pulled his prick out of her cunt and rammed it up her arse. She could feel her ass get wet with the spurting of his cum.

Isobel sobbed and moaned with a mixture of pain and pleasure. She curled over on to one side when they finished and lay recovering on a small pile of leaves by the tree.

'I loved that,' she said, still gasping for air. 'But, let's go back now. I am starting to get cold.'

'Okay,' said Sam, catching his breath. He began to rearrange his clothes. 'I'll be back shortly.'

Sam disappeared into the woods abruptly.

Isobel assumed he was going for a pee. She sat down on the tree stump as she readjusted her dress. She lit up another cigarette and waited for him patiently. It was odd that she heard his footsteps over the leaves into the forest, but then no sounds beyond that. She finished her cigarette, and decided that ten minutes must have passed. She started to wonder why he had been gone for so long.

'Come on Sam! You can't be taking that long,'

she hollered. 'What's going on in there?' She felt something slightly ominous creep over her as she shouted into the black monolith of waving trees.

There was no reply. Just the sound of the wind rushing through the trees and the distant sound of a few straggling fireworks. Isobel stood up.

'Sam, come on! I am properly freezing now. Is this a prank? Because if it is, it's a bit of a weird one. You know I wouldn't want to be out in the dark on my own without you. Come out now please. Sam ... Sam?'

Still, there was no further reply. She felt unnerved by the hollow silence that echoed back to her when she shouted into the trees. Isobel got up. She walked towards the section of the woods in the same direction that Sam had just disappeared. After a few steps, she thought better of it. Something didn't feel right to her now. She felt singularly alone standing in the woods. All that seemed to lay before her was even less light. It felt like a hopeless task.

She took a few steps into the wood and strained her eyesight to try and catch a glimpse of Sam, or any movement at all. She now began to experience a hint of worry. Perhaps he had fallen over or knocked himself out. She produced her mobile phone and sent him a text.

'Where are you?' it read.

There was no reply, and neither could she here his phone buzzing in the trees. She knew also that the heath had notoriously bad mobile phone reception. People traditionally lost each other on the heath all the time because of it. She walked back to the tree and waited a bit longer for him. Sam still failed to return. She sent him another text. This time she was slightly annoyed. She decided she was not going to be a party to what seemed like such a badly-timed ruse.

'I am going home. This is creepy. I will see you there,' she typed. She sent the message and began to walk home.

Feeling slightly crestfallen by Sam's weird prank, Isobel walked through the paths and across several fields in the direction of Parliament Hill. She descended the hill path that led down from the top of Hampstead Heath towards the direction of her flats. When she finally reached the bridge that linked the heath to the rows of terraced houses, a firm sense of relief returned to her. It felt good to be out of the darkness again. After the fireworks crowds had dispersed, the heath had a way of taking on a very dark and lonely aura. In truth, she knew there was nothing to fear in a deserted field. Very few people went up the heath after sunset without good reason. On previous visits she had seen a few groups of teenagers here and there, gathering on the benches at the lower part of the park. But this was often done to facilitate the smoking of a joint. Local teenagers would often go there to escape the prying eyes of their parents so that they could drink cans of beer or cheap wine in peace. She knew that the other side of Hampstead Heath had a reputation for being busy in a separate way. It had a very discreet gay cruising ground. All locals knew about it, and treated it rather like a wildlife reserve. It had been common knowledge for so many decades that it must have deserved one of those brown plaques of historic interest by now. But that section of the heath was a long way over, on the other side of the park. Besides, cruisy guys had their own agenda, which always involved other gay guys. They never bothered anyone. There was another piece of local history about Hampstead Heath on top of that. Locals claimed that it was haunted by highwaymen and plague victims, but she had yet to witness a real ghost. Parts of the heath could feel distinctly eerie at times. It was heavily overgrown and easy to get lost on it. At night on the heath, the rustling in the shadows coupled with the absence of light frequently made it hard to work out what all the odd noises might be. The heath could be unnerving at night, but she still found herself attracted to it.

Isobel continued to head towards home. She was still annoyed by Sam's twisted idea of a prank. It was unkind of him to leave her up on the heath alone, even if it was just for a joke. She didn't like those sorts of jokes. Sometimes, Sam could have a convoluted, base type of humour. She often felt irritated by it. He seemed to enjoy the kind of cruel jokes that only he would be able to laugh at alone. It was the kind of behaviour that led her to believe, that ultimately it would be one of the future deal-breakers for their relationship. She put that thought out of her mind, as she knew it wasn't a large enough problem to bother to decry. With that thought she reflected that there were lots of little problems like that with him that weren't big enough to decry. She tried not to let her present circumstances fuel her history of annoyance.

Isobel noticed that the lights were still on at the nearby corner shop. She thought that perhaps they had decided to stay open later due to the fireworks and the promise of some extra trade that might be milling around. She nipped in to the shop and bought another packet of cigarettes, some kitten food and a few snacks. She trudged up to her flat with the bag of groceries and unlocked her front door. Sam was concentrating on the computer with his headphones on. He was busily typing away.

'Where did you get to?' said Isobel, annoyed.

'What?' he replied, slipping off his headphones. 'What do you mean?'

'Well, you disappeared into the trees. I waited ages for you. Why didn't you reply to my texts?' huffed Isobel angrily.

'What are you talking about? I have been sitting here. In fact, I am not even sure where my phone is right now.'

Isobel picked her phone out of her bag and rang his mobile. She stared at him with a caustic glare. Sam looked back at her with confusion. The phone began to ring in the bedroom. Isobel looked at him feeling perplexed. Sam stood up from his chair to retrieve his phone from the bedroom. He looked at his texts and read them.

'What do these texts mean?' he asked.

'We were at the fireworks,' she said, 'then you took off. That was not cool, Sam. Not cool at all.'

'Isobel, no. I was not,' he said calmly. 'I have been here drinking and managing my forum all evening. You know I always do this on Friday night. If you are trying to give me shit about it, then, I don't know what to say to you. I always manage my forum and drink on Fridays. You know I am not bothered about fireworks. The crowds do my head in. So please don't try and start trouble with me about it because I didn't go.'

Sam's tone was very confrontational. He didn't seem to be getting the whole picture. Isobel glared at him in shock. She puzzled that she was going mad. Her second thought, was that he might be drawing the prank he had played on her a touch further. She paused, and momentarily wondered to herself if she had been hallucinating. She questioned if Sam might be playing an odd game with her that she wasn't fully following. She reminded herself that she had never hallucinated before. So, she concluded that it must be her second theory.

'Look,' she said bluntly. 'It was a good joke. Now it's over and we're home now. I am not getting the humour of it. If you think it's funny, well... that's up to you. But you shouldn't have left me alone on the heath like that. There's nothing funny about leaving me alone in the woods at night.'

Sam looked at her with a dumbfounded expression.

'I was NOT on the heath,' he demanded. 'I was here. If you want to look at my forum threads so you can see for yourself. I have been typing for the past two hours. I can show you. In fact, I am starting to think that it's *you* that has lost your mind. Two hours ago, you stormed out of here. You slammed the door and I am presuming you went to see the fireworks at the top of the hill. Now you are insisting I was there and that I abandoned you on the heath. But I wasn't there. Look at my thread. Either you imagined it or you are playing some sort of mind game with me, and I don't like it.' Sam's voice was calm, but she could tell that he was on the cusp of losing his temper.

He pushed the chair back from the computer and let her sit down so that she could view his thread. She settled at the computer chair and scrolled back, using the mouse. From what she could see, someone with his user name had been typing in the forum thread for close to three hours.

Isobel stared at him. She went quiet, not knowing what to think. She let out a long sigh and put her hand on his shoulder.

'Okay, let's just drop it. I am going to feed the cats and have a bath. I am cold from being out for so long,' said Isobel. 'I am too tired now to fight about all of this. You won. Enjoy your evening.

Sam didn't react. He sat down. He pushed his chair back in front of the computer, then continued typing and attending to his forum. Between them both, nothing more was said. A stand-off had been achieved as there was nothing to establish in that conversation that made any sort of sense.

Isobel entered the bathroom. She turned on the taps to draw her bath. She sat down on the toilet seat, waiting for the water to run. Unconsciously, she locked the door. She felt like some part of her needed to be alone to reflect on all the peculiar factors of that evening. She also, didn't feel like experiencing any more pranks for the night. The lock clicked loudly.

She pulled off her torn tights and wet knickers, then she removed the rest of her clothing. Now standing naked, she watched the bubbles froth up above the waterline as it filled the bathtub.

Her mind started to replay the events of the evening. She stepped carefully into the hot water and began to try to figure out what had occurred that evening. She also noticed as she got into the bathtub that she still smelled intensely of vigorous sex. 'How could he not have been there?' she posed to herself. 'How could someone she has been with for years be anyone other than the person she had been with that night?' She sunk her head beneath the water line and began to speculate in the hot water. Perhaps Sam was in possession of a type of split personality that she hadn't discovered until now. He *had* been spending way too much time indoors. That could be a factor. Perhaps he went out to the fireworks, drank blueberry gin, had sex with her in the woods and *then* his other personality forgot all about it and went home, she mused. But, that still didn't explain the forum thread. Even if he had made up a fake thread in something like a photo editing app it would have taken him hours. That theory just didn't jell right in her thoughts. The conversation thread had still been moving when she had looked over it.

She knew for certain, that the man that had been standing beside her on top of the hill that night at the fireworks, had definitely been Sam. And the wild spontaneous sex in the woods was exactly reminiscent of the kind of decadent, orgiastic fun that they used to engage in at the start of their relationship. For that short while up on the heath she briefly felt connected to him again. The feeling of being given a glimmer of hope only to have the rug pulled out from under her feet on that earthen floor filled her with a renewed sense of despair. It exasperated her to feel that moment of hope. She momentarily had a chance to believe that things might be improving, only to have them dashed by coming back home to exactly what she had left behind earlier in the evening. What had happened on the heath made her feel like they were starting to break down all the barricades and secrecies that had crept up between them over the past few years. And for a fleeting time in the dark woods, Sam had been that person that she found so exhilarating and exciting. When she first met Sam, he was full of risk. He was fun and wildly experimental. She wanted that Sam back. She looked up at the white tiles of her bathroom from the bathwater and remembered how many times they used to play in the bathroom, taking turns chaining each other to the bath taps or experimenting in water sports. She felt a shudder as she looked at the bathroom floor and thought about how many times they had resorted to fucking each other before and after their baths together. Being with him on the heath had made her remember why she loved him. Now, it just made her feel sad and confused about why he had returned to the flat without her, only to embrace the miserable demeanour he had been let himself sink into for so many years beforehand.

This was the first time in years that he had allowed himself to be so sexually unrestrained. But from the moment that she arrived home, it appeared as though he was in denial about what had happened between them on the heath. She concluded that either he had lost his mind, or she had. Either way, she decided that this was not a productive state of affairs.

Isobel felt aggrieved by her thoughts. It all seemed so illusory and unhinged. Nothing was adding up. Her mind was struggling to recount the details of what had actually happened that evening. If he was claiming he hadn't been on the hill, then he was either gas-lighting her or he was pursuing an elaborate prank. Sam had a history of gas lighting her, so that was plausible. He had a manipulative way of telling her she was crazy if she tried to protest about anything he had done previously that was counterproductive for either her or both of them. On the other hand, she wondered if this all had been a fleeting hallucination. She resolved that if Sam was in denial about their activities on the heath, then he must have somehow disconnected himself in some way from reality. She looked at the pile of her torn clothes and her underwear as it lay on the bathroom floor. The physical evidence of the night was telling her a very different story, and it was a highly conflicting one. It made her feel like storming out of the bathroom to demand he admit to everything that had happened that night. But she saw his forum thread. She felt his shoulder at the time and it had been warm. It hadn't been chilled from visiting the heath. Hers had been. His would have been as well. There was something about him that night that made her start to believe that he had truly *never* been out of the house.

She considered her second option, which involved her mind having become a stranger to her. Perhaps she imagined it all. This premise would mean that she had just spent the evening watching the fireworks with an unknown random person on the heath which she believed was Sam. This also meant that she had had sex in the woods with a someone who transpired to having been a total stranger. Isobel thought about the situation. Could she have hallucinated? She recalled their conversation on top of the heath. It had been very familiar and full of personal knowledge about their home life. He had said at the time, that he had followed her from the flat to the top of the heath. She carefully scried through her memory looking for clues, but found nothing.

Isobel was distracted when she heard a scratching at the bathroom door. She unlocked it and opened it slightly. Two small kittens walked into the bathroom. They jumped onto the toilet seat and peered over the rim of the bathtub to survey her strange immersion in the bathwater.

'Hey guys,' said Isobel with a sorrowful lilt.

'I will feed you in a minute. Then we are going to bed,' she said to them.

One of them mouthed a tiny meow but no sound came out.

Isobel got out of the bath and dressed in a towel. She sat down on the bed and opened her laptop. Aimlessly, she checked through her social media pages. She clicked on the links about Parliament Hill to see if anyone had uploaded any good pictures of the fireworks. She then remembered the photographs she had taken. She made a mental note to upload them in the morning at the same page. As she clicked through the images, she noticed something strange. An image of her had been captured in the background of another person's group photographs. She could see herself clearly smiling whilst smoking a cigarette. She recognised herself as being in conversation with someone else in the photograph. Except, in the space where the person she was talking to *should* be; was instead a red shard of light.

A few of the pictures showed strange, wispy flashes of light and bubbles. They looked to her like it could have been caused by either have been the reflection of miniscule raindrops or dust. Isobel noticed that the figure she had been talking to. The person in the photographs was certainly the same shape and size as Sam. The part of the photograph where Sam should have been seemed unusually blurred compared, whereas there was a sharper focus on the part of the photo that she was in.

It was a bit strange to look at. She was aware photography was often very hit-and-miss in the dark. This was especially the case when the backdrop was surrounded by fireworks and mini rockets. It just seemed odd to her he was blurry in the photograph and she was not.

She carried on looking through the pictures on the

page. Further down, she found another image of herself in the background of a different photograph. This time it she off to the right. The space where Sam should have been standing was more centred in the image. Isobel looked at the humanoid black shape that was illuminated against a backdrop of a group of people lighting a sky lantern. The black shape was standing there, not Sam. She spotted two tiny points of red showed up in the same space approximately where the figures eyes should have been. Isobel felt a racing in her belly. She remembered that group on the heath. She also clearly remembered that that was about the same time that Sam had approached and stood beside her. But in the photograph, what she saw that she seemed to be conversing with, was just a tall, black shape.

Isobel began to furiously search through the rest of the pics. There weren't many to choose from. The tail end of the few photos that had been uploaded showed one small image of Isobel and the black shape standing in the background behind a group of people holding Roman candles. Isobel saw herself immediately in the picture. Her body was turned in conversation, clearly facing the red eyed, black shape. Her breath slowed. To anyone else, it could easily have been misconstrued as a blurry background. But to her, she knew something was wrong. On one hand, it confirmed to her that she had been there. It was certain that she had been conversing with someone shaped like Sam. He was also about the same height. Beyond that, she had no other information. The situation was puzzling.

She stared again at the images for a few minutes. None of it was conclusive. Nothing made sense. Then, having decided that she was too tired to carry on speculating what had happened, she dressed for bed.

She walked back into the living room.

'I am a bit tired. I am going to go to bed,' she announced to Sam. She lifted her pair of kittens and kissed Sam on the top of his head, conveying a form of 'Goodnight' to him.

He didn't look up from the screen. He just carried on typing, giggling and drinking.

'Yeah,' he said. 'Good night. I will come to bed later. I am in the middle of decimating a troll.'

'Okay,' she sighed. 'Maybe see you later.'

The next morning, Isobel woke up alone in her bed. She walked through to the living room and saw Sam asleep on the sofa. He had covered himself in a blue and black afghan blanket that she had knitted. She had made it out of boredom during the previous winter. She didn't really like that blanket now.

She settled down at their shared computer. It was where he had spent the night before typing away in his chatrooms. In the first window that she opened, were the messages from his forum. It seemed careless of him to leave his second window open. It showed he had been exchanging messages with another girl. He messages showed that he been spending part of the night flirting and chatting her up. This wasn't the first time she had seen this kind of behaviour from him either. Several times she had found him cruising 'discreet liaison' types of websites. In the times that she tried to confront him about it, he would have flatly denied it all. She also had a nagging doubt about every time she had gone away to visit family. She was aware that Sam had been out, hooking up with random people behind her back. He never answered his phone when she went away, and he was always so much nicer to her when she came back. It led her to decide to set up a few covert profiles on those sites when she felt certain he was lying to her. He always took the bait. She would then arrange to meet him via the profile, then never show up. Isobel felt a pang of misery fill her heart. She pushed it down and left it never to be addressed as it was less painful than facing the truth. It was another one of those glaring problems that she had with Sam that was now, too late to bother to decry.

Isobel experienced a moment of gnawing, unspeakable lowness about what she had just experienced. That lowness didn't feel like a freshly opened wound or perhaps the dull pain of a familiar, settled scar. To her, the pain was similar in likeness to a small recess in a rock face above the sea. The pain felt like a kind of small hollow in the rocks that generations of birds had been aware of and had sought to nest in for the past few centuries. Sam's latest offensive of 'covert activities' had been wielding their axe of destruction in her mind in a particularly battering manner in the past few months. Sam had been spending more time carrying out various forms of secretive internet behaviour. When he was asleep she would explore deep into the different names and sites he had created for himself. He never knew she had full knowledge of them. When she was done looking at what and who he had been pursuing, she would wipe all the history searches and let him carry on lying to her. She tried to understand why he felt the need for attention from women other than herself. She had tried a lot of ways to try to mentally combat the way it made her feel. But in the end, she knew it was because somewhere along the way he didn't care about them as a couple. She was just convenient for him. He loved her free flat and free money. She even said to him once, 'The minute you know you don't love me anymore, just go. It's less offensive than staying.' But he always answered that he *did* love her, so there was nothing she could say. The situation was incredibly depressing. She didn't seem to be able to move forward or back.

In the back of her mind, she knew she wasn't the right woman for him. At first, she knew he was dazzled and intrigued by her eccentricities. But as time went on the truth was that he was destined to fall into line with everyone else's sense of what was expected in a standard couple. In this era, love, to a lot of people seemed to be somewhat like a business deal. Passion seemed to be an extinct concept. It wasn't the case for Isobel, but it felt like that from Sam. If she had been the right one for him, he would never have felt the need to chase strangers on the internet. He knew had a girl that loved him, that was right there beside him. It was soul destroying to her that she knew that had no value to him. In the past, she had racked her brains about how to try to behave, dress and look more acceptable and normal, so she would be blameless as the acting 'perfect partner' for him. After a long spate of trying to change into someone else, she realised that she just wasn't that fake person at all. And those efforts she made to maintain an equilibrium in the relationship only resulted in making her even more unhappy, so she gave up. The worst part of their situation was that she still loved him. She knew Sam knew that, and because of it, he would psychotically use that love as a stick to beat her with. Isobel knew she had fallen deeply into a trap of putting all their problems to one side. The goal results she truly desired was just for everything to be okay between them from one day to the next. Now, every day was just another day of having a go at patching up the crumbling tower of their situation.

Isobel stared at the thread and thought about it again. If he had been sitting typing on his thread all night and drinking: there was no tangible way that the Sam she had been on the heath with could have been the same person.

She closed the window and dressed in a short black dress. She lit up a further cigarette to give her the courage to face the day, then headed quietly out of the flat in the direction of her favourite coffee shop.

It was still very early in the morning in London, but it was nice to be out in the fresh air. The past few months of being shut in a flat that was beginning to feel like a tomb with only Sam's negativity to listen to had been very disheartening. He spent most of his time as a shut in, staring at the computer. She didn't like being in her flat very much. It could be a negative depressing space, full of negative comments from Sam. She had experienced many days in exile from her home when he acted like that. The only impetus left for being there was to be with her kittens. If she was in one room, Sam was in the other. She knew in her heart everything was falling apart. It *had* fallen apart. But despite the facts, her inner stubbornness never wanted to let go of the first few months of real happiness they had had when they were first together. Isobel felt a nostalgia and a sense of loyalty to those few good times they had had. She dearly wished they would just come back.

She strolled over the road to her local café. She ordered coffee and found an empty table on the pavement outside. As far as the previous day was concerned, nothing about it was yet coherent.

Chapter 2 The Walk

'Well, I've got my coffee and it's portable,' Isobel thought to herself. 'So, it wouldn't hurt for me to do a little trip back up the heath again to retrace my steps. Whether Sam was or wasn't there, doesn't really matter to me right now. What I think I need to know is whether I was at that tree alone or not. There must be something there. There must be some footprints or some evidence. For my own sanity, I need to see the site in broad daylight.'

Isobel stood up from the table and began to head for the route that would return her to the top of Parliament hill. Still drinking coffee and puffing away at her cigarette, she began to wend her way up to the top of the summit. She could feel the same cool wind rushing through the trees, gently chilling her face.

She walked past dozens of terraced houses and noticed various people buzzing around through the windows as she passed them. Most of the people seemed to be getting ready for work.

She reached the top of the road. She saw the trees and grass of the heath begin to appear before her. Her own last step resounded on the pavement and transferred to the soft earthen pathway that led to the top of Parliament Hill. A few locals were mulling around.

Residents walked their dogs. A stressed-out looking jogger fled past her. Isobel made a concerted stomp up the last few feet of the dirt path until she reached the viewpoint. She stopped to try to visually recall what had happened that night before on Parliament hill. She began to play it over in her mind. She stood on the spot where she had been and remembered the placement of the crowds. She had seen them all laughing and chatting. She looked around. Empty bottles of wine, spent fireworks and other random bits of detritus littered the grass from the night before. Nothing looked out of the ordinary. She couldn't see anything particularly out of place compared to any other fireworks nights she had spent on the heath. She stopped to look over the views of London for a moment, then turned to head towards the wooded paths that she believed she had walked along with Sam on the previous night.

As she retraced her steps her mind began to wander. She thought about all those houses she had walked past and the people that had been bustling about inside of them as they got ready for work, school or wherever they had all been rushing to get to. She thought about the several hundred people that had been gathered on the heath the night before. It was an odd feeling to live in London sometimes. There were eight million residents and most of the time they seemed to try their hardest not to acknowledge each other. That was the most bizarre thing about living in London: the unwritten rule of mass facelessness. Isobel thought about a prison drama she had once seen that involved inmates avoiding eye contact with each other. In London, on the tube trains and on the street, everyone endeavoured to conduct themselves in the exact same way. It was hard for deal with sometimes, because she had grown up in a small village. She was used to people being a great deal friendlier than they were in this vast metropolis.

As she continued to walk, she thought about the city's population. There had been times in the past when she had felt a degree of camaraderie with different friends in the same locale as her. She thought about her friends, her ex partners and people she may have only known for a short while. There was a surface transience that loomed over the general consciousness of London. She acknowledged the massive amount of people coming and going to and from the city. She found their mass inexplicable desire to be invisible to each other strangely unnatural. She surmised that they made no eye contact with each other because they wanted their own space. But then, why go to a space with eight million people in it and want that? There was no way of knowing what length of time these people she had seen for fleeting moments throughout London would know their compatriots, but sometimes, she caught herself trying to read the relationships between strangers, just to see if there were any patterns forming in her observations. She too, had been involved in situations that she felt confident at the time would last forever that seemed very secure. But even those situations would disintegrate for some reason. It was at that point that she felt more informed about the way London worked. No matter how solid a situation could be, it was a fact that neither she nor any former companions would know anything more about each other's future. Being part of London could be a very strange thing.

It meant that one day, two strangers could meet and possibly fall in love, then another day down the line they could break apart to the point that they would not even know the day the other one would die. To her, that was the essence of what made London feel so anonymous. For a time, the care was there. At another point in time there would be no care at all. Humans could be very hard to understand.

When Isobel first came to London, she believed that big cities were places where people would want to be friendly with each other, seeing as they made a conscious decision to be in the company of so many people. But it quickly transpired for her, that this wasn't to be the case.

London was often too fast to be totally friendly. It was crammed full of people all intent on commerce. It felt more like a collection of dragonflies swarming around a pond, or a vignette of endless windows stocked with random people experiencing various personal dramas to a dialogue you could never hear. The crux of her line of thought was the realisation that there had been a time when she and Sam had been strangers to each other. Then they met, fell in love and started a life together. Now they were living together and had regressed back being strangers to each other once again. The previous night had briefly changed that. Even though it had been sexual, it was the first instance for many months or possibly years that she hadn't felt alone. She stopped by the bridge and looked down at the view of the pond below.

Isobel felt certain that they both had stood there the night before. She remembered having taken a big glug of that blueberry gin. She remembered how warm it made her feel. It felt far too real to allow herself to believe she had imagined it all. Standing there made it hard to figure out what had happened the night before. She took solace in the fact that she knew she had the will to find the answer. London was a gargantuan and surreal city at times. It was often commonplace for inexplicable things to happen. When inexplicable things did happen there, the reasons behind them would frequently be explainable. She knew that this situation, would be explainable too.

Isobel carried on walking. Eventually, she stopped at where she had been sitting by the tree stump. She sat there and looked around on the earth floor. She tried to see if there were any recent footprints or markings that would help cement the activities of the night before, but it looked like the earth had been too heavily impacted to tell. The years of thousands of foot prints caused by joggers and dog walkers taking the paths had packed any chance of new markings down. Isobel stood up and walked behind the tree. Beside it's massive root system was a large, human-sized hole. It was inside of the tree near the base. The aperture was just large enough to fit a person inside the tree. She felt suitably curious enough to enter the strange tree to see what was inside. Upon entering, she noticed how the roots inside of this tree were shiny from more years of wear and tear from people's visits to its interior. She looked up inside the tree and wondered how it managed to stay alive with no middle. Not finding anywhere comfortable to sit inside of the tree, she opted to perch against a flat bit of a smoothed-out tree root. She looked up again. At the very pinnacle of the trees interior she spied a set of what looked like a carved collection of tiny circles. To see them at first, she had to tense up her vision. They were barely noticeable. She produced her mobile phone and focussed the camera on the circles, then zoomed in. She photographed the circles and looked down at the picture on her phone. It was hard to make out what the symbols meant. They seemed to have grown as part of the roots rather than having been drawn or carved in. She thought that it might be a little bit of simulacra or something similar. She posed the idea to herself that the tree may have just decided to grow that way. In nature, anything was plausible.

Seeing nothing interesting inside the tree beyond the strange tree symbols, Isobel felt no further forward in understanding what had happened. So, she elected that she may as well go home. She was aware that she was out of both coffee and cigarettes, and it was too early in the morning for her to stay like that. She clambered haphazardly out of the large hole at the base of the tree, nearly tripping as she exited the hollow.

Sam was leaning against an opposite tree with arms folded. He was smiling from ear to ear. She stopped, with eyes widened at the reality of his standing there. It seemed he was indeed quite real. She walked over to him, and poked him in the belly.

'So, you are real?' she said in a quizzical fashion.

'Yes, that's my stomach,' he replied.

'But clearly, you are not Sam. I left him asleep on the sofa, and there is historically no getting him out of bed at this time of the morning. You look exactly like him, in every way. Who are you?'

'I'm with you,' he stated. 'I am whatever you want to see,' he replied enigmatically.

'Are you some sort of ghost or the devil … or something like that? I have read about that sort of thing,' said Isobel thoughtfully.

'Well, yes, and no. I am both and neither,' he laughed. 'Besides, you'd never get the devil out here, not at at this time of the year. He's almost always in a meeting these days and he tends to go on holiday either in China or the middle east. I have got his number, but it's not on speed dial. He gets a bit cranky if you phone him without good reason.'

'I see,' said Isobel with a grin of disbelief. 'I suppose I would be more alarmed by this whole doppelgänger experience if I weren't in weirdy London and I hadn't already shagged you senseless last night. But it rather takes the shock out of a situation, all that carnality.'

'Baby, you can have me any time you like,' said the entity.

'Good, I will!' she said with a half-smile.

'Good,' he answered. 'But you know, you shouldn't have taken a picture of the inside of that tree. It's only going to cause a lot of problems. You photographers are too observant for your own good. You know I thought I had hidden that quite well. But you snagged it on the first go.'

'Why, what is it?' quizzed Isobel.

'Well, what do I get if I tell you?' he said with a sly smile.

'What do you want?' she countered with a naughty tone of voice.

'Hmm, actually, there *are* a few things you can give me and there *are* also, a few things I can give you as well. That's why I became attached to you in the first place.'

'I see,' Isobel replied. "Attached," she copied. 'Do tell. What do you want and what are you going to give me, then?' she quipped.

'Well I would like a more permanent place to live. I have been getting by on random energy here and there and it's not been enough for me. I want Sam's body. And you can give it to me.'

Even though the conversation seemed to be turning towards sounding somewhat insane, Isobel decided to pursue it, she was interested to gather information and find an answer to the previous night. She continued.

'Hey, you and me both!' she laughed. 'He used to be a lot of fun, then he got boring. I was not aware that I can make his body available to you. But if I am, then … let's talk. What's the deal on the table?' she joked. 'The first thing I will need to know, is what I am going to get out of it. And the second, is how do I not know you aren't going to turn him into some sort of mass-murdering, zombie-based, baby-eating genocidal maniac?'

The entity laughed. He spoke to her softly.

'I just want a little more time on the earth. And there just happens to be enough suspension of disbelief in you to let me manifest for a while. You're a little bit shiny to me, you know. You also seem to pick up on the drill of most things quite swiftly. That's useful to me. I can work with that. I have a few errands to run in this locale. So, what do you say? Do you fancy a gamble?'

'Well,' continued Isobel with a smile of accommodating disbelief. 'How long would you be possessing Sam's body for?'

'That would be, until my errands are done,' he answered.

Isobel looked at him with impatience.

'You know; I don't mind playing games. I quite enjoy them in fact. But, this negotiation is going to happen a lot more smoothly if you *tell* me what your plans are. Are these errands you speak of for something good, or evil?' she said. 'I need to know all the facts so I can give an informed "yes" or "no". Isobel's playful tone generated an air of make-believe to the conversation.

The entity let out a long sigh.

'Those words, "good" and "evil" are considered very old-fashioned phrases where I come from. Things are not black and white. Look around you. Is this world black and white? No. It's multi-coloured and that's for a reason. Things are not all good or all evil. In truth, God and the devil resolved their differences a long time ago. If anything, they both now see mankind as their common enemy.'

Isobel looked up at the sky to think about what he had just said. She felt faintly delighted by the concept that she might be allowed to sign her boyfriend's body over to an ambiguous entity who would live with her for a while, and possibly be carrying out errands that may cause a new fabric of change. She noted to herself the other option that it may also cause havoc on a mass scale. She felt a mixture of complete and total disbelief coupled with a desire for something new to happen. She resolved that the potential for mayhem was of little consequence considering all things. She was intrigued, thinking at the very least it would be fun to entertain the concept for a little while longer.

At the same time, she thought about the great sex she had experienced the night before. And she thought about how boring Sam had become and she visualized him sleeping off a hangover, back at home on her sofa. She smiled. If she made this decision, it would be based on instant gratification. But these were the times she found herself living in. Besides, the Sam that was currently asleep on the sofa in her flat, hadn't exactly furnished her with a great deal of incentive to protect him from such influences.

'Okay,' she said. 'Let's just say that hypothetically, I go along with your plan. You haven't really outlined what I get out of it, besides some great sex. You get something that is useful to you. And yes, I get some great sex and that's very useful to me. But I think I am going to need a bit of a sweetener in case you turn into some sort of possessed black demonic form, midway through this deal. However, now that I think about that, that's kind of hot too.'

'Well what do you want?' he asked plainly.

'I want love, I want money, I want freedom. I want autonomy. I need a new car and a new wardrobe. I need a bigger place to live in. I want a garden for my kittens. I'd like to go to the Maldives. I mean I haven't lain on a beach in 7 years. That sod never makes any money and I am skint out of my mind. In fact, he's into to me for twenty-three grand. In short, I'd like a little more success in life. I'd like to be happy. I'd like some excitement. I'd like to not be bored with a boring person. The monotony of my life is driving me insane to the point of envying the dead. If you can change that, then we might have a deal.'

'Ha, sounds like you have had a little time to think this through,' said the entity. 'And if you say he owes you; then you are in a position to sell the debt on, are you not?'

Isobel's eyes looked up towards the top left corner of her brain as she thought. She frowned and raised one eyebrow over this concept.

'Hmm… Well, I guess I have had five years to consider all the shortcomings caused by my own stubborn smoke screen around this shitty relationship. He's kind of fucked up my life and everything that could have gone with that. The things that I have listed for the trade are not of immense importance to me. They're not. But at least I will have something to show for my losses. I highly doubt it that the things I requested will make me entirely happy on their own. To be truthful, there isn't really any material object that is going to fix the time I have wasted. I don't think much of it will mean a lot to me, but I would like to find out for myself if it would or not. I am aware that these things would only be fulfilling on the surface, for a short while. The thing that I lack the most, is the feeling of some form of admission. I want to be allowed to participate in life. I know nothing about that and I feel nothing from it. And, just because I haven't had it doesn't mean I have learned to live without it. That's why I am comfortable negotiating with you in this bizarre fashion. I mean, the way you arrived last night still seems a little bit unreal to me. But frankly, I don't care what road leads to Rome. I just want to go to Rome.'

'Hmm,' said the entity. 'I can make a lot happen for you, if you help me. You might find my need of your energy a little bit draining at first. But once you get used to it, you will hardly feel it at all. I can assure you a positive difference in Sam. I can make all the things about him that you found dull will be soon gone. The more you come to appreciate me, the higher the grade of energy I will be able to receive from you. Therefore, it is in my interests to please you. Overall, it's a pretty harmonious trade-off from where I am standing.'

Isobel looked at him pointedly.

'And tell me this, what are these pressing errands that you need to do so badly that you are prepared to give me some of the things in life I have had to do without? Are they that important?'

'Well, my errands are of a personal matter,' he replied. 'You will know when I have done them. I can confirm that they won't do any damage to you personally.'

'Or my cats?' she threw in.

'No, of course not!' he blared. 'I have very little to do with the animal world. I deal strictly with humans and human type beings only.'

"Hmm, human-type beings," Isobel copied. 'That's a bloody strange concept to think about, and even weirder to say.'

'I am a reasonable person,' he stated. 'So, I will give you until one a.m. tonight to think it over. If you want to make the trade, come back here and see me. I have just enough energy to keep going until then. If you aren't here by one a.m., I will have to make different arrangements in another district or another world. For my part, I think you should say "yes". However, I will be fair. I will allow you time to think it over.'

Isobel took very invading step toward him. 'Yes. I'd like to mull it over.' She moved towards the entity and kissed him in a lascivious manner. 'I don't really know you. But I also wonder what I really have to lose. I expect I will be back later, probably,' she said with a wry smile.

'Do you play chess Isobel?' the entity said.

'Sometimes, yes, I do,' she replied. 'What is your point?'

'What you need to do today, is figure out, whether you want to play chess with me. And if you want to whittle that idea down a bit more, ask yourself whether or not you want to play at all. That should make your thoughts about this situation easier to work through. Life is about risk. Perhaps it's time you took a new one.'

'Thanks,' she said. His words seared through her mind.

The entity put his hand out in an offering for her to shake it. Isobel instead grabbed his ass.

'Catch you later, stranger!' she said with a chuckle.

Isobel walked away. She left the Sam-shaped entity standing beside the tree. She turned back to take one last look at him. He was still there. He smiled at her. She felt a little surge of excitement. The previous night's sex had been indeed, spectacular. She could feel a blush begin to warm across her face. All things aside, this confirmed that she had recently engaged in woodland rampant sex with a total stranger. The realisation made her feel slightly wobbly with glee.

She returned to the bridge, then meandered across the paths through the forest walkways. She smiled as she took in the morning sunlight and thought of these new developments. The entire experience made her decide to herself that she *did* want to play. She knew had already made the decision in her mind from the moment she saw him. He was everything she wanted. He had managed to capture everything she loved and lusted about Sam without the caveat of torment that accompanied his mundane, daily negativity. This new person was abound with mystery and a dark glamour that she could feel herself growing to crave. Neither did he seem to have psychological battlements up around him like the ones that made her feel like a stranger when she was at home with the regular Sam at the flat. She knew it Would be a gamble. It felt like a mad, one-shot deal. But so many times before, she had let unique opportunities slip through her fingers. Ten times out of ten they were opportunities missed because they would keep the peace with everyone in her sphere. She mused that she didn't know the real consequences of taking such a risk with this stranger. But, what she *did* know was what the consequences of maintaining the status quo would be. This choice would be about risking the unknown to escape monotony.

Something Isobel had read a long time ago was some platitude about the definition of insanity being the act of repeating the same thing over, yet still expecting something to change. Yet, that statement applied to this new situation. There was no reason to not explore the possibilities. Then again, she thought, what about real Sam? Was he that bad of a boyfriend that he deserved to be handed over to the stranger as a vessel for a set of undisclosed errands?

'Yes', she decided, 'he was'. But, to be decent Isobel came to a conclusion. She decided that she would be democratic about this by giving him the rest of the day to prove her wrong.

She stopped at the top of Parliament Hill and looked in the direction of her building. She could see the stretched line of white flats with their endless hallways leading to many anonymous domiciles. She looked at all the further buildings that stretched beyond hers into the distance. They led all the way down to the River Thames and beyond.

'This is a strange town', she thought.

Isobel was resolute. When she got back she would see if she could change anything in her boyfriend Sam at all. She decided she would be straight with him. She would give him one day to try and prove that he was not worth this so-called possession or whatever it was. If he proved to redeem himself even a little bit, she decided wouldn't go back to the tree. That seemed like a very fair shout to her.

Isobel strolled down the hill. She stepped off the heath and then returned to the café that was across from her flats. She bought two more coffees. She chose a different type of coffee for herself and a black one with lots of sugar for Sam, in the hope that it would help wake him up.

She crossed the street and re-entered her building, thinking about what to say to him. Indian bells rattled on the front door as she walked into her flat. Her two kittens, Jupiter and Mercury, scrambled to their battle stations to greet her. She put the two coffee cups down. She picked up Mercury and gave him a kiss. Sam laying snoozing on the sofa. He was just as she had left him. She attempted to gently wake him up by prodding at his shoulder.

'Hey sleepy. It's nearly noon. I brought you some coffee,' she said in a musical tone.

Sam grunted.

' Mrrhrhph,' he said.

'Come on Sam! The sun is shining. The world is out there. It's waiting for us to go do something today. Let's go out!' she said optimistically.

Sam yawned and rolled over.

Isobel picked up Jupiter the kitten and put it on top of him.

'There's hot coffee here, and an alarm cat,' she said inflexibly. You have no excuse to not wake up.'

Sam countered with a drawn out, growling yawn.

'I don't want to get up. I have a hangover. There's nothing out there. I'm tired. Leave me alone. I am not in. I am still asleep,' he replied gruffly. His barrage of excuses was very dismissive of her optimism.

'Well, *I* want you to get up. *I* want your company today. I want us to go out and find something to do! It doesn't even matter what we do. I just don't want another day to pass that is the same as yesterday and the day before. Come on Sam! You're a young man! Let's go do something!' Isobel held out the cup of coffee for him to retrieve.

Sam grabbed the cup of coffee from her hand. He pulled the kitten along with the coffee under the blanket. 'I do want to 'do something'. I want to go back to sleep after I have had this coffee and had a go on petting this cat.'

'Well, that's very admirable. But unless we do

something interesting today. I am sorry to report that the rest of our future together is going to go to hell in a hand basket. I mean, I don't mean to be flippant about it. But I am just going to politely ask you to get your shit together for me today, or we are going to have to rethink this relationship.'

Sam threw the covers off and sat up.

'Oh thanks. Wake me up with coffee and a cat, then 5 minutes later we are back to the ultimatum. If you want me to go. I will go!' he roared.

'No, Sam. I don't and never wanted you to go. I wanted you to come out of your cocoon and be a butterfly. I don't know if you have noticed but for this past 5 years you have gradually become a shut-in. You live in front of the computer and spend all your time ignoring me. You do absolutely fuck all to progress our life together. You could find a job to help me with the rent and bills. I love you Sam, but you have made our life together unfuckingworkable. All I am saying, is PLEASE, PLEASE get up, come out and do something constructive with me today so that I can feel like we are still in the land of the living. That's all I am asking for. Come on, Sam.'

Sam huffed. He sat up and lit a cigarette.

'You know I was up all night on my forum?'

'Yeah, I know,' she answered, sighing. She

knew that he was about to come out with another bullshit statement that would extract him from having to do anything interesting with her for yet another day.

'Well I am still tired. Maybe if you let me sleep for a few more hours we could go out a bit later,' he said.

She almost believed he meant it.

But in truth, Sam had just achieved another fob-off statement that was going to see another day fly by. She knew that they weren't going to go out later when he said things like that, as he had said that exact thing to her numerous times before. She knew he would sleep for another two or three hours and then spend two hours on the computer. By the time he would be ready to announce they could go out it would be 5 o'clock. It was like a fucking merry-go-round the level of pain in the ass he could be. She felt like she could kick herself with the level of manipulation she had given in to with him over the past five years.

Isobel sat down on the edge of the sofa beside him.

'I tell you what Sam, think of it like this. You're a good-looking bloke. You're tall, you're blonde. You're smart. You came out top of your class in the country. You are a great lover when you want to be. You have the mental faculties and looks that would have made you a viable candidate to invade a small South American country if you had so desired. But you don't seem to want to use those embellishments and gifts. Those are the things that made me fall in love with you in the first place. It's been a long time since you used them. Even if I wasn't here and I didn't have my little business for us to fall back on, what would you do if I got hit by a bus tomorrow? What would you be doing with your life? You know, you're 31. What in life is really stopping you from being happy and using all the talents you were given?' She studied his face with concern, waiting for a response.

Sam puffed on his cigarette and sipped his coffee. He stared at her without giving an answer.

'Sam, I am going to give you an hour to wake up,' stated Isobel. 'I want you to make a plan for us for something to do today. That's all I can say. You have a lot going for you. I have always said that. But if you don't want to use what you were given. Then we are going to have a severe problem, starting from right now.'

Sam took another puff from his cigarette belligerently.

Isobel walked out of the room. She entered the bathroom and slammed the door. Her head swirled with ire.

'Okay,' she thought to herself. 'I can give him 45 minutes to pull himself together. In fact, I can give him and hour and a bit. That's no problem. And if he does pull himself together and we do go out, then maybe we can get things between us back on track. I wonder if I should tell him about my trip up the heath? I mean, if I told him the truth would anything be any different? Or would it just end up being another drawn-out conversation about the fact that everything that I had a problem with about our relationship was just something he believed I was conjuring up in my mind?' Isobel knew the mental territory of his stubbornness to change a bit too well. She decided not to bring the subject up.

Sam had a way of wheedling out of situations by convincing Isobel that she was either, constantly in the wrong or hormonally crazy.

It was for this reason that Isobel decided that it was a conversation not worth bothering to have. It would be better to just see if he got the hell out of bed, went outside with her and pursued just about anything outside of this flat. She would have been more than happy to have any remote kind of proof that he wasn't basically, a living corpse. Isobel exited the bathroom and went into the bedroom.

She opened her laptop and took a long look at those pictures from the social media pages from the night before. She looked again at her talking to the black form in the pictures from the fireworks. She saw something in her own eyes that she hadn't felt in a long time. It looked like she was having fun.

In truth, she knew Sam wasn't going to get up and go

out with her. But, being as fair as she could be, she confirmed to herself that she would wait the hour. She would see what he was like after a few cigarettes and maybe another coffee. For years, her relationship with him had been dragging her backwards. She was always excited about getting up and doing something with her day. Whereas most of the time she had spent with Sam was like a fight to get him motivated to even get out of bed. And she had long given up about asking him to get a job. She had kept this charade, clinging to the hope that everything would work out okay. It never was. He never came back to being the person she fell in love with. She experienced a moment of lament about the waste of it all.

The hour passed quickly as Isobel caught up with her internet check-ins. She shut the computer down and walked through to the living room. Sam was sitting in front of his computer terminal, typing in conversation to another person.

'So, are we going out? Have you made a plan?' she asked patiently.

'Well I looked around the listings and there's nothing really on today. Can we do something tomorrow instead?' he replied.

Isobel sat on the sofa deflated. She knew she had just been bullshitted yet again. 'Round and around in circles, here we go,' she thought.

'I don't think so Sam. I don't think we will be able to do anything tomorrow. I think time will be up by then. What about maybe heading into Camden for a gig tonight, at least? Why don't we do that?'

'What? And go out with all those drunks in the street? Who would want to go into Camden on a Saturday night with all those chavs and teenagers? What would be fun about that?' he said.

'Well it's better than nothing. I feel cooped up in here.' Her tone of voice became very glum.

'Well you go out then! You go!' he said confrontationally. 'I don't want to go. I hate Camden.'

'If you hate Camden so much then why do you live here?' she said. 'Oh God. Just forget it, Sam.'

Isobel went into the bedroom and shut the door, she threw herself under the covers and closed her eyes. Another day, and another circular argument lost. She was sick of the whole dance. She felt weary of the rigmarole of never going anywhere and never doing anything. She also resented the constant undertone being made to feel unwelcome in her own flat. If anyone was a stranger at this place, it was her.

Isobel thought back to the entity. How much havoc could he really cause compared to the shit she had been enduring for the past 5 years? Even if he decimated the whole of North London, it couldn't be worse than the monotonous boredom of living with the miserable shit bomb that she had so foolishly shacked up with. She had a better chance of happiness with Jack the Ripper than the directionless misery guts out there in the living room. It made her angry that he was blindly frittering his life away as he typed on his plastic monkey keyboard. She was furious just thinking about it.

Isobel's thought about everything that had led up to the past 24 hours. She realised that this decision was no contest. In truth, Sam had no practical use for his body or and even less for his brain. In his present circumstances, she believed that the entity would probably achieve a lot more on the earth being Sam, than Sam ever would.

A mass of swirling conflict manifested inside of Isobel's brain. She settled in her bed. All that thinking about it all made her tired. She drifted off to sleep. She woke up a few hours later in the blackness of her bedroom.

'What time is it?' she called thought to the living room. She could hear Sam typing. He stopped for a second to answer her.

'It's nearly ten p.m.' he replied.

Isobel quickly got out of bed and dressed in her coat and boots.

'Right then,' she said. 'I am going to that gig.'

Isobel walked out of the door and headed back for the tree on the heath. She didn't kiss Sam goodbye.

Chapter 3 The Deal

Isobel arrived an hour earlier than arranged at the tree. But it didn't matter to her. She felt that it was better to be an hour early than to get there 5 minutes late and miss her chance. She sat by the tree roots and looked at her phone. There were a few irate texts from Sam. She looked at them but just pushed the thread of those conversations out of her mind. They had the slightly incendiary tone to them. One text read "Enjoy your gig," and the other said: "Thanks for taking off."

'More bullshit, more control,' she thought.

Sam's incessant manipulation and laziness had her fed up with him. The only time she really felt comfortable with herself, was when she was away from him. It made her sad to think about the way things were now.

The constant day- to-day struggle of trying to get him up off his arse was, for Isobel, often too much to bear. And perhaps the new stranger might be full of problems. But new twists and turns were part of the package of what coming to live in London had been about to Isobel in the first place. London was, like the stranger said one big "game of chess". London was a place where you came to play chess with your life. For Isobel, London turned out to be one of the hardest games of chess she could have played. It didn't matter to her anymore if she had to start another game from scratch.

Isobel turned. She saw the stranger emerge from beneath a canopy of lightless trees.

'You're early,' she said.

'And you were earlier,' he replied.

'Well, you must have known as I walked away this morning that my mind was already 90% made up.'

He sat down on the tree roots beside her.

'You seem to be taking this all in your stride Miss Cumont, Miss Invisible Isobel,' he quipped.

'As are you,' she answered tentatively.

'What have you been doing Miss Isobel, whilst you have been sitting here?'

Isobel stubbed out her cigarette and smiled at him devilishly.

'I have been thinking about sitting on your face, mostly. Let's just say things didn't go very well back home,' she answered with a sardonic glare.

'I know Isobel. I have been there all along,' replied the entity. 'I saw you sleeping. I saw you get up and go out. You gave him every chance. It's the same chance you gave him every day for the past 5 years. I can assure you I will make far better use of his brain, body and incidentally his girlfriend than he ever could have.'

'How long have you been there?' said Isobel.

'Since the seed of dissent was awakened in you. It was really a combination of things. But there's also an old portal in your house.'

'What?! Where?' she laughed. 'Is it in the cupboard? What? Is it in the cat box or under the sink? What portal is there?'

'Sam is the portal. He's been sitting at the computer for so long, soaking up everything that is positive and negative off the internet like a sponge. He's like an open door to anything and everything that wants to come through. His activities have been like a duck shoot for certain other world presences from the get go, I'll be the first to admit it. I will also add that I am certain that I am a much better option for possession before another creature gets inside of him. I had to fight my way to the front to stop something more stupid and destructive from getting in. That's out there too. But I guess my will is a little bit stronger than the others, because they have backed off. This situation has been positively optimal for me. He's got the looks and the brains. He's even got the hot girlfriend. But his spirit is weak. The only will he has left belongs to you now. By letting you drive everything, he failed to see that he also gave up his right to his own soul. All I need, is your blessing. Then, everything can change.'

'Well, I have thought about it and I trust my decision. I have decided I have nothing left to lose. He's already driven away all my friends and family with his shitty behaviour. All I have left is him and he barely acknowledges me. It's no prize. So, no. I don't care what you do with him now. You have my blessing. Just tell me what we have to do to make it happen.'

'It's nearly one a.m.' he said. The stranger produced a book bound in black velvet and a white feather quill pen.'

'All you will need is the little sharp fruit knife that you keep in your bag, and your telephone,' he said directly.

Isobel produced the items from her bag.

'Prick your finger with the knife, then copy out the sigils from the tree that you photographed on your phone. Write it in your blood into this book.'

Isobel winced and cut her finger open. The stranger cupped his hands and caught the few drops of blood as they dripped from her hand. She dipped the feather quill in the ink and began to copy the sigils from the photograph into the book. She used the light from her phone.

'I forgot my phone had a light. You know, this seems all a bit too easy. But I am guessing it's really not.' She said as she wrote.

'Correct. That is exactly correct,' said the entity. 'What we are doing right now is the combination of your mind made up mixed with the deployment of the correct set of directives. I'll tell you right now, if you weren't so capable of making up your mind; the copying of those sigils would be meaningless. When one partner is weak and the other one is strong, that's the optimal time for people like me to make a move. Although, I do have some important matters to attend to. I will reward you in ways you will appreciate. Don't worry about that.'

'I am still trying to feel guilty about signing him over to all of this. But really, I also struggle to care that much. I keep trying to have some form of compassion for him, but I feel strongly that he's brought it all on himself,' said Isobel reflectively.

'Will he ever get his body back? Will the original Sam return?' said Isobel as she wrote.

'Ask yourself,' he countered. 'Do you really want him to? Have you ever seen such a waste of human life? Don't you think that anyone or anything inhabiting his body could make better use of it than him? He's been staring at a computer all day long for half a decade doing absolutely fuck all. He's a fucking effort and you know it. If you didn't, you wouldn't have been so quick to fill out the forms.'

'I am not a big one for guilt and remorse. I always accept responsibility for what I have done and will do. I let him get that way. I let it happen. However, I am also un-letting it get that way and un-letting it happen right now. So, you take him. At the end of the day, he's pretty much my property. I have fed and clothed him, paid the rent and bills. I have kept him for 5 years. There is nothing materially belonging to him that hasn't been produced without a direct action from me. And yeah, I do feel a little bit of a sense of entitlement to improve him, even if that means ripping out his soul and giving him a new one. Fuck him for the way he's been with me. I don't care what you do with him. Do your best. Do your worst. You have his body to live in with my blessing. Just please, all I ask is that you don't turn into him. I'd rather risk it with a stranger than bear another day like this.'

Isobel went quiet and carefully copied the remainder of the sigils into the black velvet book with the rest of the blood that she had dripped into the stranger's palm.

'Good,' he said with satisfying tone. 'Thank fuck for that. Now we just have to let the symbols dry and we are good to go.'

'How long should that take?' she queried.

'Long enough for you to sit on my face,' he said with a diabolical grin.

'That seems reasonable,' Isobel countered. 'I am starting to like this arrangement already.'

Isobel knelt down in front of the stranger. She felt the damp earth and sticks digging into her knees. Within seconds she was deep-throating his cock.

There was the strangest imagery darting through her mind during this chilly night on the heath. The unfamiliarity was an instant turn-on. She felt she was in a trance-like state of distraction. Tiny bursts of light, like fireworks would form behind her closed eyelids. When she opened her eyes, she would catch a glimpse of strangely beautiful demonic and angelic-looking figures, as they raced past her peripheral vision.

She stopped what she was doing. She looked up at the stranger and looked at him with a little bit of curiosity. It was mixed with uncertainty.

'Do you like this as much as I do?' she said.

'Such a question,' he replied.

The entity stood Isobel up and hugged her. 'You know what I have seen up to now? You have spent so long with someone who has been going out of their way to convince you that you were crazy. His weaknesses made him try convince you that everything that was wrong in your situation, was all your fault. And it's now amusingly ironic that his gaslighting of you has made aspects of your psyche so divorced from reality, that it has made other things on alternate astral planes now possible for you. Sam should have stuck to reality. He brought all this shit on himself. There was never anything wrong with you. You did nothing wrong.'

'Well, it's just that every time I wanted to do anything sexual with him, he acted like it was a chore. I found it difficult, that lack of enthusiasm. It felt for a long time like there was no point in bothering any more. I mean, I spent so long clinging on to the person he was. I guess I have known for a long time he's been gone and isn't coming back. This seems like just a formality now.'

'Which is what also made your new path choice so very easy,' he said softly. 'Ah! The ink is dry now. It must be the fresh air! And I now feel ludicrously fantastic! I feel so full of life.' The stranger drew in a full breath of what sounded like his first real lung full of the November night air.

He took the phone from her hand, turned on the light and looked at the velvet book. He checked over the drawing.

'It looks perfect,' he said. 'That was helpful.

Thank you, Isobel. Now let's go back to the flat.'

'What about the book?' she replied.

'It goes back inside the tree.' The stranger walked over to the hollow of the tree and tossed the black velvet book inside.

Isobel followed him to look inside and see where the book had landed.

'What if someone finds it?' she said.

'The only person who can find it, is you. Because Isobel, it's only visible, to you,' he laughed.

Isobel took the stranger by the hand and they walked across the heath back to the flat.
She went quiet as her mind began to process what was currently happening. She wondered what would be the result of two Sams being in her flat when she got back. She also wondered that she may have totally lost her mind finally. If that was a fact, she could hardly bring herself to care at this juncture. Sam at home had been driving her bug-fuck for years. The really was nothing left to lose.

She turned to the stranger as they tramped over the long grass on the shadowy heath.

'Are there going to be two "Sam's when we get home? Is there going to be some sort of mortal battle round the kittens, when we get back in? Am I going to have to chop up bodies? This is all been left hanging in the air, you know,' said Isobel, giving her best poker face.

The stranger laughed.

'Call me Samn, now. S-a-m-n. That way, no one else will hear anything different. But you will. And no, Sam won't be there for long. When we get back to your domicile all will be revealed. The chopping up of carrion will not be required.'

'Okay, so I have to just wait and see what happens?' quizzed Isobel.

'Well it's happened. If you let me go into the flat for a minute or two before you, I will step into his body. It's pretty easy from here on, this business,' replied Samn.

'There's no mess and no fuss! Plus, you can finally switch that twattish internet off for the first time in who knows how long. You can forget all about that negative little sod. I am going to change a lot of things for you, Isobel. But the only thing I can't change, is the time you lost. You are going to have to find a way to resolve that in your head on your own. We've done the deal. It's going to be beneficial all round. I have some errands and you can help me with that. I always do what I say I am going to do.'

'You didn't say anything before about me helping you with your errands,' she retorted.

'Isobel, I get my energy from you. I got my body from you. In many ways, I belong to you. Yes, I have a will of my own. But I am out of my own world and traversing through yours. I am going to need you as a guide. So, I don't think that's a lot to ask, considering what I have to offer.'

'No, it isn't.' she said cheerfully. 'And I did say I was up for a game of chess, after all.'

The two exited the foot of the heath and made their way through the silent streets past a row of terraced houses and found themselves outside of her block of flats. They walked quietly up to her front door. Isobel unlocked the front door in as ninja-like a manner as she could. She watched with surprise as her two kittens bounded to the front door, irrespective of her stealth.

She quietly swung the door open and ushered the stranger in.

He put his finger to his lips. 'Give me three minutes, then come in.'

Isobel waited by the front door. She stared at the ground and clasped her arms around herself. She could hear Sam's chair being pushed back from the desk. Then she saw a flash of red light emanate from the hallway that led to the living room. She continued to listen. She heard heavy footfalls advance inside the flat. The two cats turned tail from the front door and scampered off into the bedroom. Isobel pushed the door open slightly wider, in an attempt to hear any other noise. She heard the computer being switched off.

'Come in Isobel,' said the stranger softly. It's new Samn. It's ok.'

'Ok,' she replied tentatively. 'So, where is old Sam?'

'He's mostly in the symbols of that book in the tree,' replied Samn. 'But part of him is stored on your computer. In fact, you might want to back your computer up, if you think it's necessary.'

'Well, I will have to think about that,' said Isobel sarcastically. 'Right now, part of me just wants to chuck the whole frigging thing in the bin. But I expect I won't.'

He sat down on the sofa.

'I admit this has transition has been a bit more draining than I have remembered it to be. Is it okay if I have a bath? I need to wash all of this portal grime off.'

'You may, by all means,' she replied. 'Be my

guest.'

'Join me,' he said.

'I'd love to,' she added with a glee.

Samn and Isobel walked into the bathroom. They both began to undress. Isobel turned on the taps. Hot water spluttered forcefully from the spigot. Isobel heard a faint scratching at the door. The kittens were just outside. They were sniffing around, trying to get in to the bathroom. She opened the door. Isobel knelt down and took turns stroking her cats individually.

'Not now, little kittens. I will see you in a while.' she said, shutting the door again.

She turned on the taps and filled the bathtub with hot water. Samn held her close to him and put his arms around her.

'Thank you, Isobel,' he said.' You don't know how much you have already helped me. I was waiting for the right chance for a long time. I am so glad you said yes about this.'

'Will the other Sam be all right?' she asked. There was a lilt of concern in her speech.

'Well, think of him like someone currently in suspended animation. He's not unlike a moth in a cocoon or a bee trapped in amber. He's not entirely conscious but neither is he dead. There's no noticeable difference being made to him in his life right now. I wouldn't worry about him too much. He is still doing everything he used to do. It's just on another plane of existence. It's also the same zombiesque bullshit he was doing here. The only difference is that you don't have to experience the torment of it. Don't think about him. After all, he never really thought about you. Give it time. You'll get used to this. It's going to be all right.'

'So, he's not really like a bee trapped in amber.' replied Isobel. 'Because a bee trapped in amber *is* dead.'

'Isobel,' said Samn affectionately. 'A bee trapped in amber has more life in it than he ever had. Come on now. I assure you that he's completely tucked safely away. And If you must know what's happening over there, nosey, it's that I have created a loop for him which is kind of like a mental fog. What I have done is sampled 180 of the most familiar and random days that you two have had together over the last 5 years. They are now being played back to him. As far as he knows, it's just another day. Due to the monotony of his choice of existence, it should be a very long time before he notices any difference.'

Isobel smiled at him suspiciously.

'Can that work? I guess it can!' she exclaimed.

The two stepped into the bath.

'Hey,' she said. 'Can you drink? I have some wine we could have that I have been saving for a special occasion. Want some?' Isobel stepped out of the bath and walked naked into the kitchen. She produced a bottle of champagne that she had stored at the back of the cupboard. She uncorked the bottle and filled two glasses. She returned to the bathroom and handed him a glass. Unceremoniously, she plonked down in the water at her end of the bath. She held out her glass. He clinked it with his.

'To the unknown,' she stated.

'To the unknown,' he confirmed.

Samn sipped his wine and sighed.

'This is great,' he reflected. 'I have air in my lungs again. I am drinking champagne and sitting in a hot bath with an even hotter naked girl. This is the kind of shit I would never have taken for granted. We can both start over, fresh tomorrow.'

Isobel looked at him with a frown.

'I have to go back to work tomorrow. I have a meeting.'

'Cancel it! Tell them you are sick. Tell them you are pregnant, or dead, or both. Tell them whatever you want. Tomorrow, we have plans.'

'What kind of plans? I must keep running my business. I must keep trying to pay off my debts. It's going to take me years to dig myself out of the debts he racked up for me.'

'Tonight, we sleep. Tomorrow, we clear the decks. I know where there's plenty of money and we can sort out all those little aggravations relatively easily. It's going to happen inside of the next few days. I like to keep my word. Besides, we don't need your good energy wasted on petty details, do we? I need all your energy for better things.'

Isobel raised her eyebrow. 'Oh really?'

'Yes. Don't see me as an interloper. See me as someone who has been watching you for a long time. I remember early on when you and old Sam used to get wild in this very bathroom. Back then, I was truly a green-eyed devil. I would be lying to not admit that that was not the minute I knew it would be worth changing places with him. So yes, you are going to have to lay off some of your duties for the next few days. We'll have to make a list of whatever immediate stuff is bothering you, then I am going to have to hothouse you in assisting me.'

'Does this mean I am going to be like some sort of magician's assistant?' she laughed. 'Do I get a sparkly costume?'

'Only if you insist,' Samn smirked. 'You will look a lot less conspicuous if you dress in your normal clothes.'

■■■

The next morning Isobel woke up beside her new Samn. She felt mildly surprised. He was still there and still real. The biggest giveaway that he wasn't the old Sam was the fact that he was asleep in the bed beside her. Nine nights out of ten the old Sam would be on the internet all night, cruising, flirting and downloading porn. He never came to bed. Still half asleep, she marvelled at the thought that somehow, she had somehow found a way of making that constant source of irritation obliterated from her present. 'Who cared if he was trapped in amber somewhere,' she thought. It's not like a missing person's report was going to be filed. For all intents and purposes, Samn was still here.'

She crept into the kitchen and started to make breakfast.

'Halt what you are doing,' announced Sam, 'Just get ready. We are going out for breakfast. Domestic drudgery is banned for the moment.'

'Alright,' replied Isobel.

Isobel dressed in a little black dress and heels. It felt good. She felt good. Samn dressed in a checked shirt and some faded ripped jeans.

'You look hot! Let's get started,' she beamed.

'Okay,' said Samn. He produced a set of car keys. 'We may as well drive.'

Locking the door and walking out to the front of the flats were rows of parked cars. As it was London, there were dozens of cars in the street.

'Yeah, even my kind has trouble finding a parking space,' he mentioned.

They walked a few streets along until they stopped beside a very low, open topped black car with colour shifting paint.

'A jag?' screamed Isobel with delight. 'This is my favourite car ever!'

'It's not just your favourite car any more, it's your car. It's in your name. It's yours now. I jiggled the paperwork too. I even scored you some low ass insurance for it. Let's just say I am owed a lot of favours in a lot of places.'

'Fan-fucking-tastic! I am not sure whether you are a devil or an angel, now.'

'Neither,' he smiled. 'I am self-representing really. I work for myself.'

Isobel half frowned. 'Erm, that's a bit of a mysterious thing to say. I can see we are going to have a lot to discuss about that in the coming days. But for now, where are we heading to?'

Sam opened the driver's door and ushered Isobel into the car. He shut it and went around to sit in the passenger seat. Isobel ran her hands over the steering wheel.

'This is fucking amazing! I have perved over this car so many times in so many ways. It's like a leopard! It's light and fast. Thank you. I am overwhelmed. I am finding it hard to take it all in.'

Samn smiled at her. 'You'll have plenty of time to take it all in. Save that for later. Let's get some breakfast so we can get to work. Take us to that French café at the top of Highgate Hill that you used to go to. I have missed food. I feel like I am starving. After that, we need to hit the cemetery. That's got to be our first stop.'

Isobel parked the car after finding a space on a nearby road. Samn and Isobel got out of the car and started to walk in the direction of the café.

'I feel like I want to eat everything!' said Samn, enthusiastically.

'I have no issue with that,' she replied. 'I felt

like that when visited America once. I gained 7 pounds over a two-week stay. There's just a million weird things to eat, but you never have enough luggage allowance to bring them all back to London. I ended up gorging myself full of cloyingly sweet, rainbow-coloured snacks. It was such a guilty pleasure at the time. So just have whatever you want.'

'One of the best kinds, guilty pleasures,' replied Samn. 'There's nothing wrong with that.'

'I mean, if I lived there all the time, I would probably be the size of an articulated lorry because of the unbridled colour wheel of convenience food they have over there. Everything over there is so vast compared to London. You must already know this if you have been attached to me for so much time. This French café, though, is the only place within a 5-mile radius that can cook a rare steak. They do the best steak and eggs.'

'Sounds like a plan,' said Samn.

After breakfast, the went back to the car. They drove a short distance and parked by the gates of Highgate Cemetery. It was a vast Victorian hillside cemetery known for housing almost two hundred and fifty thousand graves. Sorrowful looking statues lined the entranceway flanked by grandiose above-ground tombs. An imposing gothic chapel loomed by the entrance gates.

'I feel wobbly,' he said.

'Yeah, you were voracious at breakfast,' Isobel countered. 'But I don't think there was any way around that. I think steak, eggs, brandy, coffee, croissants and a side order of pommes frites was quite a lot to eat for breakfast. It may have disagreed with your new body a wee bit. But I didn't want to be a killjoy. Give it time, it will all go down eventually.'

'I think it will take a few days before the whole food thing will balance out,' huffed Samn. 'I just couldn't stop myself for a few minutes there.

'So here we are at the cemetery.' Isobel looked at Samn with a bemused look. 'What are we doing? Are we visiting someone? Are we making a deposit, or a withdrawal? What's the drill?'

'You'll see. Follow me,' Samn replied.

'I find cemeteries quite horny,' she added.

'You really are a pervert. Do you know that?' he said.

Samn rolled his eyes and grabbed Isobel's hand as they strolled through the sumptuous landscape of the overgrown, ivy-covered park. Unusual looking monuments lined the walkways. Black and white magpies fluttered about in the trees above. A small flock of long -escaped and now established wild green parrots called out to each other in the highest parts of the trees. The two strolled down the paved pathway to the quietest part of the cemetery. Samn seemed to know exactly where he wanted to go, so Isobel followed beside him. He stopped beside a concrete-framed grave. An ivy-covered angel stood watch above it. She was holding a down-turned torch. There was a very mournful look on the statue's face. Even though Highgate was a place of sorrow and loss, Isobel still thought it was a beautiful part of the city.

'And this is where we solve the first of your conundrums. We get your money problems off the checklist,' he said cryptically.

'Why? Are we going to become wealthy body snatchers?' asked Isobel with an inquisitive smile.

'No, we are going to become archaeologists. If we quietly dig up a section behind the far corner of this grave, I will have something useful for you to play with,' countered Samn.

'You already have something useful for me to play with,' Isobel mumbled under her breath.

'I heard that!' laughed Samn.

Isobel watched as Samn began to dig. She produced her pocket knife and began to help Samn by using the implement as a small digging tool.

'Be careful with that. You don't want to stab the money now do you?' said Samn.

'There's money in there?' exclaimed Isobel.

'Yes, oh yes,' came his reply. 'It's just about a foot down in the soil.'

'Is it yours?'

'It is now! A former associate of mine buried it there some time ago, just before his incarceration. He won't be getting out any time soon. So, there's really fuck all he can do about it. I saw him bury it, but he didn't know I was watching. So, I don't see the harm.'

Samn pulled a large grey plastic envelope the size of a ream of paper from the corner of the grave. It had been double wrapped in heavy transparent plastic and gaffer tape. He pulled a corner open. Isobel looked inside and saw a stack of £100 pound notes peeking through.

'Is this one of the errands you needed to do?' she said.

'Well, no. This is just something I am doing to free you up a little bit. I have my own specific errand list, but I just happened to remember that this was here and thought it might come in useful. I didn't really like my former associate. He could make some interesting things happen, but he spent too much time making all kinds of rainbow statement promises. He would never execute the work we needed to get done. It will be funny someday when he comes back looking for this money, because it won't be here. Which is much like the work he promised he would do with me.'

'I think I love you,' said Isobel.

'Good. If it helps us get on with what we need to do, then that's a good thing. It's a kind of alien concept to me, money, but that doesn't mean I can't watch your back, my girl.'

The two stood up over the grave. Isobel picked a flower from a rhododendron bush and placed it in the hand of the angel statue. They discreetly carried their plastic-covered package of money back to the car. As they walked through the lanes to exit the cemetery, Isobel could feel a surge of excitement flowing through her.

'I feel like today isn't real,' she said.

'It is, and so far, so good,' replied Samn. 'Now we are going to need to make a trip South of the river. We need some supplies.'

'Where to?' said Isobel.

'There's a Haitian voodoo shop in Brixton. We need to drop in there and get stocked up.'

'I actually know the one you mean. But there is a

quieter one on this side of the river. It's not Haitian, but they sell the same products.'

'Well, let's check that one out then,' said Samn.

Samn opened the boot of the car and unceremoniously dumped the parcel of money in the trunk. Isobel looked around with a culpable grin to see if anyone was watching them. There was no one nearby. Samn lifted out a few of the notes.

'Yeah, I think maybe taking a convertible jaguar south of the river that has its' boot stuffed full of money might be a tiny bit of a bad idea,' countered Isobel. 'Let's try the north of the river shop first. I suspect we can get everything that you need from there just the same.'

The two sped along the backroads of North London. They headed towards the spiritual shop. It was tucked away on a very inconspicuous street. Its frontage looked more like a perfumery. The shop was flanked on either side by a hairdresser and a bakery.

'You know,' said Isobel. 'Nothing dramatically bad has happened yet. I was kind of waiting to see if there was going to be a sting in your tail. But so far, it's been plain sailing. So, my question is this. Where is the sting in your tail?'

'No sting,' said Samn. 'For you, there's no

sting in my tail. You're helping me. What would I have to gain by screwing you over? You know part of the problem is the years of negativity you spent with that cunt in the tree. He really was killing your spirit. He has left you fearing the worst. You have to try and let that go.'

'Sometimes, I really don't know where you got the reserves from to fight it,' said Samn reflectively. 'I guess that's what I always found so attractive about you. Well, that, plus the fact that you have a really kinky streak that you hardly bother to mask.'

The two pulled up and parked the car in a small side street near the shop.

Above the shop was a sign written in simple black on white writing. It was very stylised but quietly understated. The sign read "DARK & LIGHT". Isobel entered the shop first, followed closely by Sam. It was a small shop made up entirely of tall shelves. On the first row of shelves were tall jar candles in a variety of differing colours and combinations. Above them were more candles that had been shaped into small statues. Some of the candles were shaped like black cats. Another row comprised of black skulls, whilst another offered candles shaped like two entwined lovers, depicted in red. The jar candles were covered in different spells and wishes with corresponding pictures of devils, saints or magic squares. On the opposite side of the shop were the same rows of tall shelves, but they housed a row of aerosol sprays, floor washes and incense. All of them had some type of voodoo purpose attached to them. Samn approached one wall that was full of bagged and dried herbs.

'Yeah, we need this,' he said.

A middle-eastern looking man approached them from behind the counter bearing a little shopping basket. He was dressed in a very kitsch-looking cowboy shirt.

'Let me know if there's anything specific you need,' he said with a helpful smile.

The man returned to the back part of the shop. It was divided by a chained curtain.
Isobel watched him as he sat down at a little desk. He resumed what he had been doing before, which seemed to be the act of pouring different liquids and oils into little bottles and marking them with labels. She watched as he wrote out a few labels and stuck them to the different small brown bottles. He looked up at her and smiled.

Samn began to take one packet of everything from the wall of dried and bagged herbs. He walked over to the room spray shelf and picked up three canisters, then began picking out some of the coloured candles. Isobel noticed that he chose two of every colour available.

'Do we really need all of this?' said Isobel.

'Yes, of course we do,' said Sam positively. 'If

you want a precise answer, then yes, we do, and no, we don't. We do, in the sense that this will help us get into the right head space to make things happen. That's why we are here. If we had years to fritter away, we could achieve our tasks without any these oils, candles or herbs. But for now, this is the fastest route to getting the job done.'

'Oh,' said Isobel. 'Well, lead on then, Maestro. You learn something new every day, I guess.'

Chapter 4 Freedom

Isobel and Samn lugged ten blue plastic carrier bags back to the car. They were stuffed full of herbs, oils, unusual types of incense and strangely shaped candles. What wouldn't fit in the tiny boot was stored in the foot well on the passenger side of the jaguar.

'We're not really done yet,' Samn said, closing the car door. 'In fact, we really could have done with spending more time back at that cemetery.'

'There's another little graveyard near here. Would that do? It's near a park,' replied Isobel.

'Yes, that sounds interesting,' said Samn.

They started away from the car in the direction of the park. Isobel turned around. She went back to unlock the boot of the car.

'Let's takes a some more money. Just in case we need it,' she said pragmatically.

'What would we need money in a park or cemetery for?' said Samn with a curious brow.

'In London, you need money every fucking where you go. It's costs practically £50 quid just to step outside the front door for ten minutes,' she replied.

'I will take your word for it,' added Samn. 'It's not something I had noticed before I got here properly, but I admit I haven't been totally paying attention to this reality for a while.'

'Yeah,' retorted Isobel. 'We are going to have a conversation about that sometime. Remind me to ask you where you came from, how long you've been away and why you smell a bit like pine needles, dirt and wet leaves. I mean it's a nice scent. But I have been wondering a bit what all that's about.'

Isobel pulled a pair of £100 pound notes from the boot of the car. She locked it up again. She stuffed a few of the notes down her bra, absent-mindedly. The two began walking.

'Where to, first? Are we going to the Park or the cemetery?' asked Isobel.

'Let's do the park first,' he replied.

She grabbed his hand and the two strode towards the entrance of the North London Park. A few young women with pushchairs lolled past, followed by a dog walker with 4 small, fluffy white dogs in tow.

They stopped beside a pond. She watched as Samn surveyed along the edges of the pond. Then she watched as he walked to the edge and picked up a small snail.

'We aren't going to hurt the snail, are we?'

'No!' laughed Sam. 'It's just been a long time since I had a chance to look at one properly and I like them. You know, my kind and snails have a lot in common.'

'You mean you're a one-footed hermaphrodite?' smiled Isobel.

'No,' he briefly chuckled, then caught his breath. 'My kind and snails are very similar in a way. We go about this earth, silently attending to our own world. People hardly notice us. They don't really know how or where we are born, how long we live or when our time to be alive gets extinguished. The only reason you are seeing this little snail right now is because I took the time to pick it up and show it to you. Otherwise, we would have walked through the park and not given this tiny little being any of our attention. As insignificant as this little creature may seem to be, it can still eat through concrete and reproduce itself 800 times over if it wants to. That's more than a human can do. That aside, my main point is. If you don't look, you won't see.'

'Well, it's a good thing I have you here to show me around my own city,' she said. There was a little bit of sarcasm in her voice but she decided to pull it back a bit. In this situation, it would be an inventive idea to let him go about the process of showing her around her own town. She inherently knew that in this situation she would probably gain a lot more by listening to his observations.

He put the snail back down beside the little pond and they walked on.

'So, I just need a few basic natural things. I need some thorns, some leaf samples and a few flat pieces of rock. I also need some dirt from the graveyard.'

Isobel pointed. 'There's the churchyard over there. Shall we go there?'

Samn nodded yes.

The two walked in the direction of the tiny Victorian churchyard. Sam stopped outside the front door of the church. He looked at Isobel. 'Can you pick some of those yew berries and leaves for me?' he directed.

'I just need to pop inside here for a minute,'

Isobel did as she was asked. She soon followed him into the church. She looked in amazement as he was cupping handfuls of water from the font and swallowing it.

A calm looking monk in long brown robes approached the pair. Isobel shrunk into her shoes on the spot, feeling a little embarrassed. She imagined that the monk was thinking they were a pair of nutters who had wandered in off the street.

'You know,' started the monk.' I have read about people drinking holy water but I have never seen it done.' His tone of voice was very calm.

'Have you ever tried it?' replied Samn.

'Well I never thought to, really. I remember reading that they used to give it to plague victims, or people suffering from various ailments. Other people historically claimed it gave them visions or could make them see angels. But then, the use of it varies from country to country. Unless, of course, you were just thirsty. There's no harm done. You are welcome,' said the Monk with a serene smile.

Isobel was taken aback by the monk's accepting and non-confrontational attitude. In London, she thought that he must have been witness to all manner of loonies passing through this district. She thought that perhaps over time, he had just learned not to let much of anything phase him, and that his acceptance of Samn's actions were part of his vocational training. He had a tremendous bubble of tranquillity surrounding him. It was quite remarkable.

'Do you think I might be able to take some of this water with me?' asked Samn boldly.

'Of course,' said the Monk. 'I might have an empty water bottle in the sacristy. I'll go get it. I will be right back.'

He walked back towards the couple and began to fill the water bottle, using a gold-coloured ladle.

'I hope it's useful to you.' he whispered.

Isobel looked at the Monk and was little bit flustered. 'Thank you. I hope it will be too,'
Samn whispered back. He put his hand out and shook the monk's hand.

'Thank you, that was kind of you,' Samn took the water bottle and headed for the exit.

Isobel walked out of the door behind him.

'Well that was weird. The other night you were saying that God and the devil were outdated concepts. Now you are glugging down holy water. I can't say I really understand.'

'It's simple. Most of these religious sites are built on even older ones. I could sense that this church had been built on top of a spring. That type of water is helpful to me. That's all there is to it. I'll show you how to use it later. Besides, it didn't seem like he minded very much. It's not like he asked for an explanation. Those sorts of spiritual people never do. I could sense that from him even before I entered the building. His kind will always just let people be.'

'I thought you might burst into flames or something if you walked into a church,' said Isobel. 'I thought maybe a church might be off-limits for someone like you.'

'We really are going to have to have a long talk at some point, you know. You really are a bit mixed up about all of this business, aren't you?' Samn ran his hand over her head to stroke her long hair.

'You know, you really are a beautiful woman, but there's a few things we still need to get straightened out. Now let's head back to the car.' Isobel craned her neck upwards to kiss him on the cheek.

'Well, all relationships have teething problems,' said Isobel thoughtfully.

The two returned to the car. They got in, and sped towards home. They parked the car and then removed their shopping bags from the boot. They walk back towards their flat. They went inside and put all the new shopping bags on the counter in the kitchen.

'You know, Samn, new Samn ... weird, sexy stranger Samn,' said Isobel merrily. 'I've been cooped up for a long time in this flat. I have mostly felt alone. And it's occurred to me that perhaps it has been the same for you, wherever you have been. I can't even begin to fathom where that might be, but I noticed by the way you were eating breakfast that maybe you have been missing out on a lot yourself. It made me feel like you needed a little extra time get some life back inside of you again. And you know, here we are in London. I am aware you have errands to run. But don't you think it might be an idea if we blew off a little bit of steam first? There's no reason why we can't.'

'What did you have in mind?' replied Samn superciliously.

'Well, I was thinking maybe we could take a day to go out, have some drinks in a casino, get hammered, rent a hotel room, do a few clubs, then shag like rabbits after. Ten hours max.'

Samn looked at her curiously and scratched his head. 'You know, I have been obsessing about just getting back on to this plane and getting my errands completed for so long, that I have forgotten all those options were available.'

'Well, I have been consumed with boredom for so long, that that was the first opportunity that came to mind. That was the first thing I thought of from the minute you informed us we had a little bit of cash to play with. I think we should go and do something silly and reckless, before we go to do something serious. It will take the edge off. I have felt oppressed for such a length of time, and it would be nice to feel like myself again. Plus, it's nice to create new memories. There was nothing ever mundane enough about me that I was going to be happy stuck indoors with what's-his-name.'

Samn picked up one of the kittens and stroked her. He looked out the window. He looked at the buildings as they stretched over miles of, London until they disappeared into the horizon.

'I'll feed the kittens. You pick out something nice to wear, and we'll head into town. I don't see how one night is going to drag us that far backwards. '

'Well yeah, the one thing about London that I love and have always loved is the anonymity of the city. It doesn't matter what you do. No one cares. In the wrong light, it's a lonely city. But in the right light, it's a playground. Let's use it for that.'
Isobel made one last check on the flat and kittens. She grabbed the little bag she had packed. They locked the door and headed out into London.

'Let's walk,' said Isobel. 'We aren't far from Camden. Let's go there first, then head into town.'

The two marched towards the clubs and bars of the high street. Huge painted figures and papier mâché sculptures loomed above the bars and shops. Artistic graffiti covered every spare wall. Huge statues of horses cropped up behind various corners. Street food sellers shouted about chicken and tried to offer it to passers-by. They watched as droves of people smarmed past them. Camden was rarely closed.

Tourists were frequently engaging a drunken party there, whether day or night.

Samn stopped outside of a party store. He looked in the window.

'I think we should go in here and become pirates. No, I think we should be zombie pirates,' he said.

'Erm, I want to be a sexy zombie pirate,' said Isobel. 'No, I want to be a murderous zombie pirate porn clown.'

'That's complicated,' said Samn.

'Let's go in and see what they have for us at short notice,' she replied.
They entered the shop. A shop worker approached them. They looked at all the party supplies around them. A neon pink bridal party were all trying on party wigs and giggling to each other. They were clearly from Manchester. They were also clearly pissed. Some of them waved plastic devil props.

'Can I help you?' said the shop worker.

'Yes, we want to be sexy murderous zombie pirate porn clowns,' said Isobel.
The shop worker laughed.

'Okay,' he answered slowly, still maintaining a

perfect poker face. 'So, do you want a full costume or just the accessories and make-up?' she asked.

'What have you got?' said Samn.

'When do you need it by?' asked the shop worker.

'It's for now,' Isobel stated.

Samn and Isobel emerged from the shop. Samn was wearing a multi-coloured clown jumpsuit, and a zombie mask. He was carrying a plastic cutlass. Isobel had chosen a sexy pirate girl outfit to wear and her face was covered in clown make-up. The shop worker had stored their regular clothes into a large shopping bag. He handed the bag to them.

'There's a cocktail bar across the street. Let's go there,' said Isobel enthusiastically.

Dressed outlandishly, they made an entrance into a vast, barnlike cocktail bar decorated with Mexican day of the dead décor. A few people in the room looked up and smiled but no one was shocked beyond that. To everyone else they were just another pair of rabble rousers out in Camden for drinks.

Isobel pulled out a large note and stood up at the bar beside Samn.

'I see it's cocktail hour. What do you

recommend?' she asked the bartender.

The bartender presented them with a long menu full of cleverly named cocktails.

'Have you got anything with straws and Roman candles?' said Isobel. 'We want something served out of a pineapple with an umbrella. We need something decadent, that also gets us pissed quickly.'

The bartender spied the pair with a bit of a mischievous glow.

'Start with a ladyboy,' he said. 'It's a Martini with tequila and grenadine, served with lipstick around the edge of the glass. It will get you geared up for some more adventurous drinks after.'

'Okay, well if it's happy hour, give us 6 of those,' said Samn.
The two clinked glasses and knocked the cocktails back in succession. Red lipstick from the glass smeared their lips a shocking shade of orangey red.

'Bigger drinks please, bar-ologist! Let's keep this going!' said Isobel. 'This is a demonic emergency piss up. Time is a factor here. New round please!'

They watched as the bartender returned with a pair of bespoke-looking pineapples, full of straws, umbrellas and booze. It looked ridiculous, but the arrival made Isobel feel happy, when she saw it. It was very loud and garish. She felt cocktails should always look like that.

'This is called the "smugglers tropical blast-off",' he said. 'Two sips and you'll think you're on a rocket headed for treasure island. Just be careful if you need to get up from your bar stool. It will give you wobbly legs and you won't know about it, until you stand up.' The two began to sip at the giant cocktail.

Isobel looked around the bar. The walls looked as though they were beginning to melt. Samn looked considerably worse for wear.

'I am already feeling pissed, Izzy.' said Samn. 'Let's get a taxi out of here,' was all he could manage to say. Isobel tipped the bartender. They attempted to exit the bar.

Isobel felt as though her legs had become marshmallows. She looked at Samn as he tried to make large, pronounced steps on the cobblestones outside of the bar. She decided the safest place for them was inside of a taxi. When she spotted one, waved her arms wildly, in an over-zealous attempt to catch the driver's attention.

The black taxi pulled up. The two entered, but Samn had trouble managing to stay on the back seat. He instead calmly opted for sitting on the floor of the taxi.

'Where to?' said the driver.

Isobel tried to sound as sober as she possibly could.

'Take us to a hotel in Central London, we don't really mind which one. Just one near the centre, close enough for us to walk into Soho.'

After a short journey through the side streets of Regent's Park, they found themselves standing in front of the forecourt of a very formal-looking hotel.

A concierge smiled and nodded his head as the drunken zombie pirates walked past in the direction of the reception desk.

'See?' said Isobel. 'London doesn't care if you are a sexy zombie pirate porn clown.
If you have money to pay them and you also don't act like a git, they really don't let anything bother them. It's a remarkable thing.'

'I never knew you could do this here.' Samn mused. 'I always thought London was highly conservative.'

'Well, yeah, maybe out in the counties it is, but it isn't here. They see anything and everything, every day,' said Isobel.

They checked in. The concierge didn't bat an eyelid as he passed over their room key. After an hour of changing, showering and a very concerted effort to sober up, the two triumphantly exited the hotel in the direction of Soho.

'I say we tour the sex shops on the way to the casino,' suggested Isobel.

'Are they not just full of old men looking at porny DVD's?' said Samn.

'Maybe in the 80's and 90's, yeah, and still maybe now, yeah a bit. But sometimes it can be fun. Some of the sex shops have some nice lingerie. I can model it for you. Or, you can model it for me, I don't really mind which way round that pans out. If someone does something to somebody today, I don't care what order it comes in,' she said with a grin.

In Soho, Isobel grabbed Samn by his arm. She pulled him through a plastic multi-coloured chain curtain entrance into a shady-looking sex shop. A few guys staring at DVD's looked up at her briefly, but quickly resumed their concentrations on the shop stock.

'Okay, there *are* guys looking at DVD's in here. You were right. But let's check out the cheap, trashy unwearable lingerie section. That's the fun part of the shop.'

A rack covered in latex and black lace lingerie was set up in a corner of the shop. Samn picked up an enormous black rubber sex toy shaped like a fist and held it out to Isobel.

'What are we buying?' he said churlishly.

Isobel picked up a black leather corset, bra and suspender set and a pair of fishnet stockings.

'By the look of it, this. In fact, if it fits I am going to wear it right now. Let's see how long you last through dinner knowing I have all this on under my dress.'

Isobel went into the changing room with the garments. She put them on. She pulled the curtain back and shouted out to Samn. She was now dressed head to toe in the corset and fishnet stockings, minus her shoes.

'Do you approve?' she said, opening and shutting the curtain again quickly. She covered her new outfit up with her daywear and slipped her black high heels on.

Samn nodded yes, enthusiastically. He turned to the man working behind the counter.

'Can you ring that up please?' He gave the cashier a cheeky smile. It was quickly returned.

Isobel strode out of the shop confidently. A small entourage of the men shopping looked up and gave them a few furtive glances as they exited the shop.

Isobel was now dressed again in her dress and wrap. But her black fishnet stockings peeped out from the knee of the dress. Her shiny black stiletto heels clacked as she walked out of the shop doorway.

Samn smiled broadly and was quick to fall in tow beside her.

'Well I guess those shops are fun, after all.' he said.

'Told you!' chimed Isobel. 'Now, I was thinking Casino drinks. However, since those cocktails, I am starting to feel hungry. And seeing as we are in the middle of Soho, why don't we find a little restaurant?' Isobel stopped beside a busy gay café in the middle of the street. She kissed Samn and rubbed one of her stockinged legs against his shin. She could tell Samn loved it, but she also enjoyed the exhibitionism of flaunting Samn to the guys sitting outside the gay café. They were eyeing Samn up.

Isobel had a fleeting thought about her and the previous Samn out walking around Soho together. Original Sam had always been a good-looking guy. He had a beautiful face, blonde hair and was six feet five. Any porn star would envy everything he had. His physical endowments weren't exactly the most important thing about him to Isobel. But Sam had had this way of defining himself as a 'porn star type'. It was intriguing at first for her to find out how that dating that type of guy would play out. She found out over the years with Sam that sometimes his type *could be* all it was cracked up to be, but at other times it did nothing to change his extremely negative self-image of himself. In the early days when they started dating, the thing she first noticed about him were the male *and* female heads he could turn when they walked down the road together. She also liked the fact that she could wear six-inch high heels and still be shorter than him. Most of her previous partners had been the same height as her. Some of them had developed a fetish for liking girls in heels to be towering over them. But Isobel still preferred taller guys. In the early months when she and Sam were still at the point of being happy together, every day involved lots of sex. At first, they both lived in a fugue of unfamiliarity with each other, with a willingness to do anything off the hook to please their individual desires. Being with original Sam was like an endless party in the beginning. But then, something negative set in to him. Isobel had never managed to work out where it came from. He started to hold an adverse view of himself, it then transferred into Sam having a negative view of her. Isobel increasingly found herself no longer in the role of his 'private porn star' as she was the initial plan. She found herself becoming his counsellor, cheerleader and flatmate. It was maddening. To be so close to having everything you could ever want in a person, only to have a gremlin come along and take your shiny new toy away. She mused about how ironic her solution had had to be for that situation.

After that time, Sam had begun to fester. He couldn't get up for a single day and try anything new. She watched him spiral downwards, seeming only to be able to repeat the same patterns on a daily basis. When Isobel wasn't working, she would endeavour to try to set up a variety of businesses for him. He would feign interest for a few days, but after the initial optimism, he would just let them go down the drain.

What Isobel felt she should have done with Sam after the orgiastic partying began to wane, was to cut him loose. She knew she should have let him out into the world on his own. Let him see the dark side of trying to make a go of life without anyone there to help him out. She wouldn't have done it to be vengeful. She knew she should have done it because she was holding him back from developing the survival skills that would have made him have enough character to be a half-decent human being. The main problem was that he had no life experience when he met her. She could see his vulnerability. It made her cut him all kinds of slack. She truly loved him, but for both, their kind of love was sadly very destructive. So, whatever plane of existence he was on now, whether it was in a conscious or unconscious state, she still hoped maybe one day he would appreciate what he had had. Nothing worth having ever comes easily. She felt a slight pang of guilt of sending him to what she construed as a type of limbo. But, if he *had* been made to believe everything was still carrying on as though 'business as usual', and he was none the wiser about his current state, she couldn't really see the harm in it. For however long this possession by new Samn was going to last, at the very least it gave her some respite from the frustrating merry-go-round that she felt she had been on with the old one.

The new Samn reminded her so much of original Sam. He had this sparkle about him that seemed excited about everything around him. She caught herself a few times observing the way he looked at everything with a spark of curiousness and delight. A few times since they had been together she had to pull him away from the strangest things. A day earlier he had stopped to stare at a spider web and asked to borrow her phone so he could take a picture of it. It made her wonder what the place he had come from must be like. She wondered if she would act the same way in his world.

But by now, all she wanted to do was to try and enjoy the small things that could be enjoyed in what surroundings that they had available to them now. London had a way of making a person accustomed to accepting the most bizarre of circumstances. Isobel didn't see a vast ocean of difference between this current weird friendship and many other situations she had been in before.

After progressing through a few small sides streets in Soho, Isobel and Samn found a small restaurant that looked about right to them. They headed in. Its' frontage was glazed with a multitude of antiquated-looking window panes that had seen better days, but the interior looked clean, simple and friendly. It was a tiny inside the restaurant. There seemed to be a lot of bustling going on. The waiter showed them to the last available table, which was beside the window. He pulled the napkins out of the wine glasses and left a wine menu on the table before attempting to walk away. Isobel quickly pulled him back and ordered the first bottle of wine from the top of the list.

'That was quick,' said Samn.

'I don't have twenty minutes to wait for a drink,' she said jovially. 'If it's over 3 years old and French it will probably be alright,' she laughed.

The waiter returned quickly and began to pour their wine as Isobel stared out of the window, watching the people buzzing around outside in the busy Soho side street.

There was a small table with two chairs placed on the pavement just outside the front door. A plant pot on the table seemed to be doubling as an ashtray.

'Cheers,' said Samn, as he clinked Isobel's full wine glass. Isobel acknowledged his clink, but found herself feeling a little bit distracted. She couldn't take her eyes away from what she was trying to see. Far away down the street, she spied the small dark body of something with glowing red eyes. It was gradually walking closer to them as it padded up the road. As it got nearer, she noticed the eyes were not red from the reflections of the lights on the street as she had originally thought it might be, and perhaps that explained why she couldn't stop staring at the figure. It didn't look quite real. The eyes of the creature were glowing red as though fused with electricity. Apart from the anomaly with its' eyes, it looked to her like a medium-sized black Labrador. The dog walked straight towards the restaurant. In its approach, it walked right up to the restaurant. It looked directly through the window at Isobel and Samn. He had an expectant look on his face. It made Isobel feel unnerved. Isobel returned the dog's stare. The dog stopped by the table and chairs on the pavement. He settled to lay down underneath the table on the street. He was now out of their range of view but right beside them, lying beside the table on the pavement outside.

Isobel looked at Samn with a face full of confusion.

'I don't know what I just saw,' she said, still full of a daydream of distraction.

Samn let out a big sigh and took a big glug of his wine. 'You're going to have to excuse me for a minute,' said Samn.

Samn stood up and walked out the front door of the restaurant. He lit up a cigarette and sat down at the table outside. Isobel couldn't quite make out what was going on, but she could hear Samn having a covert conversation with the dog. Even though the glass of the restaurant window was too thick to make out what was being said, she was certain she could hear something answering him after he spoke.

Isobel watched as Samn stood up from the table. He carried on smoking his cigarette and glared down at the dog. His face was full of irritation. Having finished his cigarette, he walked back in to the restaurant and returned to his seat at their table.

'So?' asked Isobel expectantly.

'That's Brian,' he said with an exasperated sigh in his voice.

'The dog?' asked Isobel.

'Yes,' recounted Samn. 'I didn't think that I would be seeing him. I put in a request to be left alone to attend to these errands by myself. But because I haven't stayed focussed on the plans I need to carry out for these few hours, our 'directors' have decided to send Brian to come and 'assist' me as they like to put it. In short, they don't approve of me taking tonight off. They want me to attend to what I have agreed to attend to.'

'And they sent a dog to tell you this?' said Isobel. Her face was perplexed.

'He's not always a dog. Perhaps that's the only body they could get for him at short notice.'

'So, you were talking to a dog out there?' enquired Isobel.

'Yes, I was. He's been sent to inform me about what's got to happen urgently. He also knows by when. After dinner, I think we are going to have to go back to the flat. We should take Brian with us. He'll be far too conspicuous if we don't shove him in a taxi relatively soon. We will have to stop and check out of that hotel on the way, as well.'

'I see,' replied Isobel. 'I am still trying to work out why they sent a talking dog called Brian.

'They probably sent him looking like that because I have taken incarnation of someone by the name of Sam. Back in the 70's there was a crazy guy in New York who thought a talking dog was telling him to kill everyone. At the time, this guy's neighbour *did* have a black Labrador dog. And, the dog was being possessed by Brian at the time. Brian was the real one making all the dark suggestions that the killer had been complaining about. Brian *had* been talking to the crazy guy, he was winding this bloke up. I think he just took a dislike to the guy. He can be kind of annoying like that. I remember him telling me that he took great delight in the fact that he could influence the looney guy and that the guy was never able to prove that a dog was talking to him. It was all Brian's idea. I guess the politics of what you would call 'Hell' are sometimes very confusing. Brian has a reputation on our side of things for getting a bit annoying if he is bored. He has a habit of stimulating chaos back our way when he doesn't have anything to do. So, it doesn't surprise that they have shoved him out into the work field for a bit. However, if they have sent Brian, it will be for reasons comprising of a mixture of their own sick humour coupled with a mandate to hurry me along to get my tasks done.'

'So, he's going to be coming with us?' said Isobel.

'Yeah, sorry,' replied Samn. 'He's been sent to keep an eye on me. I am not happy about it. They can be a load of ball-breakers over there sometimes.'

'Sounds like it,' said Isobel.

The two lifted their glasses and began to look over the menu. Outside, Brian continued to lie patiently under the table. In the typical style of London, the frenetic, self-absorbed passers-by failed to notice Brian's glowing red eyes as they rushed past him.

Chapter 5 The Black Dog

Even in a planned situation of deciding to take a little holiday, no one is guaranteed of getting it. You can take the phone off the hook, put your phone in a drawer and not answer the door. You can banish yourself to a part of the country with a bad internet connection or terrible phone signal so no one can find you. You can actively decide to get off the fairground ride that might be your day-to-day existence, but invariably it's times like those when some thoughtful gargoyle from the ether will decide that it's time for you to have an ordeal. Your car will break down half way up a mountain in the snow. Your friend will have a marriage crisis. One of your neighbours will have a house fire. And in that instance, all your plans for freedom will in variably have to go back in the drawer, because you are stuck being a stupid, nice person who wants to help.

Isobel had been through all those situations individually at some point in the past, so the fact that she had to hail a taxi, ingratiate herself enough with the taxi driver to let the dog go in the car, check out of a hotel room she had only been in for less than an hour and be obliged to return home was not all that surprising to her. She was always of the mind-set in London to ensure she took pleasure in trivial things, because all too often some new drama would manifest, and wreck the day. The arrival of Brian the dog was just another penny in the jar. She smiled to herself. They had to use her wrap to conceal Brian's glowing red eyes from the taxi driver. And it worked. Samn manufactured a brilliant excuse that the dog was nervous in cars. He convinced the driver that covering the dog kept him calm during car trips.

Isobel paid the taxi. She gave him a nice a tip with a smile and a polite "Thank you". She turned to Samn.

'I think it's best if we bring him inside,' she said. 'We can't leave him out here to skulk around in the bushes.'

'He doesn't have to,' said Samn. 'He knows how to stay out of the way until he's needed, if you prefer that.

'No,' sighed Isobel. 'He's still a dog and I don't want to leave him outside all night. Whatever else he is, is fine with me if he doesn't scare the kittens. I am not really bothered about him being with us, as long as he behaves.'

'I don't think he will scare the kittens. Cats know things,' replied Samn. I think that they will twig he's not really a dog quite quickly. But we'll see.'

The trio got in the lift and made their way up to the flat. The kittens were waiting at the door as Isobel, Samn and Brian the dog walked in. Isobel had expected the kittens to dive under the bed but they did the exact opposite. The first kitten jumped up onto the settee, followed by the second. They seemed to welcome the arrival of Brian with expectant curiosity.

Isobel put her keys down and went into the bedroom. She dressed in her black lounge pants and a vest and went into the kitchen. She constructed two screwdrivers out of some leftover vodka and orange that she had found in the fridge. She strolled back through to the lounge and handed one of the glasses to Samn. Isobel sat down on the couch next to the two kittens and lit a cigarette. Brian the dog sidled up to her. He cocked his head sideways, looking at her for acknowledgement. Not feeling phased by his glowing red eyes, she put her hand out and began to stroke his head.

'Does your friend drink?' said Isobel.

'Err,' laughed Samn. 'I'll ask.'

Samn led Brian into the kitchen.

Isobel could hear their two distinct voices but not quite make out what was being said. It sounded like they were speaking a foreign language. After a few minutes, Samn returned and sat beside Isobel. Brian settled on the floor beside Samn.

Isobel stared at him.

'Well, what did he say?' she laughed.

'He said he wouldn't mind a drink as well, but can wants to know if he could have it with ice, and preferably in a bowl.'

'Was he speaking another language, when you two were in there?'

'Yes, a bit,' said Samn cryptically.

Isobel got up and fixed a Samn a small vodka and orange with ice. She put it in a bowl and set it down beside Brian. He settled down in front of the bowl and began to lap it up thoughtfully.

'I think he looks tired from the journey, you know. You need to tell him that as he is a dog now, there will be no more vodka. It's not good for him.'

'That's very perceptive of you Isobel,' said Samn. 'On one hand making the transition from one plane to another is exciting because you feel an immense rush arriving somewhere new, but at the same time it drains a lot of energy from you. It time to readjust. He is feeling the same type of drain that I felt.'

'Well maybe we should go to bed and let him sleep,' said Isobel.

'We may as well, we have got a lot to do tomorrow,' nodded Samn.

Finishing their drinks. Isobel took a blanket out of the cupboard. She put it down on the living room floor for Brian to sleep on. He circled around a couple of times and settled on top of the blanket. She stroked his head again and said, 'Good night.'

Isobel and Samn sprawled out on the bed and settled under the covers.

'Sorry,' said Samn.

'It's not really your fault. At least you had the willingness to go out and try to have fun. That's a difference for me, on its own. Besides, there will be other days. It doesn't matter. It's hard to think of something amazing to do at short notice. We can do something else later.'

'I know,' purred Samn. 'Brian is probably fast asleep now. You know, there was no reason you had to take off that new corset.'

Isobel's lips curled into an impish smile. She got up and stripped naked out of her lounge pants and vest. She proceeded to redress in her new corset, stockings and high heels as Samn watched from the bed. She noticed his eyes become very glassy, as though entranced. Samn tried to stifle a yawn.

'Keeping you up, are we?' said Isobel. 'She picked up a pale purple riding crop from her dresser and used it to stroke the length of his thighs. She walked over to the edge of the bed and looked down at him and smiled as she watched his cock stand to attention.

'You know there's something I haven't told you yet about this place,' said Isobel with a teasing tone to her voice. 'Air is a very precious commodity around here.' Isobel knelt on the bed. She removed a stocking from the bedside drawer proceeded to tie it around Samn's cock and balls. She watched as they became viciously red and swollen. Isobel slowly crawled up the length of the mattress over Samn's body. She licked Sam's thighs and torso, then turned to face away from him. Nudging her knickers to one side, she manoeuvred herself into a position so she could sit on his face. She felt a surge of excitement as she felt his tongue plunge forcefully into the furthest reaches of her pussy. She felt like molten pleasure was being poured through her entire body.

Isobel picked up the riding crop. Teasing, she made a quick, sharp hit to the top of his penis. She watched with delight as his cock writhed from left to right. She momentarily lifted her ass up off of his face. She heard Samn gasping for air. She gave him a few seconds to catch his breath before lowering her pussy back down onto his face again. Using the lightest tips of her fingernails she began to scratch up and down the length of Samn's chest and legs. She knelt over and lightly kissed the tip of his cock, then raised the whip again and hit it with more force.

'You need to keep licking my pussy. If you do it correctly, I … will let you have … some more air,' moaned Isobel.

She felt Samn's tongue force it's way further into her cunt. Isobel moaned and felt dizzy. She could feel herself becoming unbearably wet. Her body began to tingle all over as her mindset began to focus on only pleasure.

Isobel raised her ass and knelt over Samn, impaling her mouth on his swollen cock. Samn gasped in shock, reaching for more air. Samn pushed his face back into her pussy as Isobel calmly directed his head towards her ass. He forcefully plunged his tongue up her ass. The sight of his red and swollen cock was too tempting for Isobel to ignore. She quickly found herself distracted by the need to impale herself on it. She crawled along the length of his body and crouched, facing away from him. Carefully, she rubbed the edge of her pussy against his cock. She could feel Samn trying to move closer to get his cock inside of her, but for a few passes she moved away from it, only lightly allowing his cock close enough to feel her wetness. The third time, she thrust herself down onto his prick and heard Samn let out a moan behind her. She repositioned herself so that she was straddled either side of his legs, whilst still facing away from him. She felt a sharp pain mixed with ecstasy as he pushed the length of his cock as far as it would go. She could feel it stabbing her somewhere near the base of her stomach. The intensity of the simultaneous pain and pleasure made her feel light headed, and her vision blurred.

She then turned around, facing him. He grabbed her and pushed her onto the bed. He held her legs to one side, before sincerely beginning to fuck her as hard as was physically possible. She stared up and looked directly into his eyes, but soon she had to shut them. The sentiment was not wasted on her, but the raw luxury of the experience caused too many senses to flare up at one. Isobel screamed loudly as she came. She couldn't stop her cunt's overwhelming reaction to squirt. She felt the bedsheets flood under her ass into a massive pool of pussy juice. Isobel found herself hyperventilating. She watched Samn cinematically as he took his cock out of her and plunge it forcefully into the side of her cheek. Warm jets of cum flooded into the back of her throat. She opened her mouth to show him and then swallowed it all with a smile.

Samn collapsed back down on the bed. Their heavy breaths soon returned to a regular pace. Isobel handed him a cigarette from a packet on the night stand and took another for herself. She lit them both. The two inhaled the cigarettes deeply. Still spaced out, Isobel looked around the room thoughtfully.

She spied a dark figure sitting quietly by a gap in the bedroom door, looking in to the room.

'Brian, you are a fucking pervert!' shouted

Isobel.

Samn leapt up and darted to the bedroom door. He shut the door in Brian's face.

'I should have guessed that would happen. Brian doesn't get out a lot. I will have a word with him in the morning about it. Sorry.'

Isobel laughed. 'It doesn't matter. I mean I would rather have not been observed by your friend. But I was too distracted to think to shut the door. It's no problem. And you know, for a little while, I forgot he was out there feigning sleep.'

'I will take that as a compliment,' said Samn.

'We should take him for a long run sometime, so we make sure the little bugger passes out properly.'

'I wish I had a better excuse for his behaviour. It's his nature to watch. He's a watcher. He's here to watch me. It just would have been nice if he had been a little bit more selective about what he should be watching. But as I said, he doesn't get out a lot.'

'Never mind, no harm done,' said Isobel as she kissed Samn on the cheek. She curled up in the crook of his arm and they both fell asleep.

The next morning Samn was awake before Isobel. He crept out into the living room and was surprised to see

Brian fast asleep with the two kittens curled up beside him. He leant down and gently shook Brian.

Brian stretched and yawned. The two kittens both perked up at the same time and tip-toed through to the kitchen.

'Is Isobel still sleeping?' said Brian.

Samn let out a large heaving sigh of exasperation. 'Yeah matey, thanks for that last night. You know I haven't been here all that long and she hardly knows me as it is. A little bit of discretion might not have gone amiss, you know.'

'I don't know what you expect. I am a watcher. I watch. That's why I am here,' replied Brian.

'Yeah, but you were not sent here to watch that!' exclaimed Samn.

'Well let's not split hairs. I am here to watch you. And I am also here to remind you we have a time frame to keep to. It was hard enough getting the directors to agree to let you come here and carry out this these tasks. And although you may think the winter equinox is an ocean of time away. You, in fact have just under two months to get it together and start the wheels turning,' retorted Brian.

'True, that's not a lot of time,' returned Samn.

Samn sighed.

'You know, taking on this dog form thing that you do is pretty weird. I don't know why you decided to take this canine guise. It makes me feel uncomfortable, chatting to a dog on this plane. Can't you possess something else for the interim?' requested Samn.

Brian lifted his back leg and scratched one of his long black ears laboriously.

'Do you think you'd look less conspicuous if I had possessed a hamster? I had to choose between being a pup or bringing out one of the hamsters. That's all that was available at the time. And I wasn't all that excited by the idea of being trodden on by a drunk in Soho whilst trying to get your attention,' replied Brian.

'Okay, point taken,' said Samn. 'But if you can find a vehicle that is a little bit more helpful in future, I would appreciate it.'

'I'll see what I can do,' replied Brian nonchalantly.

'Fine,' said Samn with a bit of irritation.

'Yes, fine. Just keep your eye on the work,' retorted Brian.

Samn stretched and walked through to the kitchen. He

opened a tin of cat food for the kittens and put the coffee machine on. He poured out two cups of coffee and went back into the bedroom, slamming the door. The kittens jumped for a moment at the sound, but quickly turned their attentions back to their cat bowls.

Samn put the two coffee cups on the night stand and crawled back into bed.
Isobel flipped over to face Samn and curled her body around him. She was still half asleep.

'Good morning,' he said quietly. 'There's coffee here.'

Isobel mumbled a half asleep "Thank you".

'It's too early,' she added.

'I know,' he replied. 'I was just taking the opportunity to go and have a word with Brian. There's a few things I needed for him to understand before this project starts to get implemented. We just have to either remember to shut the door, or not care if he watches us.'

Isobel mumbled again, 'Can't we just stay in bed for a few weeks first? I don't want to get up, ever again. Let's just stay here.'

'If I didn't have a time frame to keep to, I would be right there with you on that subject. But, I do and we do. We have a schedule and it can't be broken.'

Isobel sat up and sipped her coffee. She reached over the bed and grabbed her cigarettes.

'So, considering "The Watcher" is in the next room watching everything you do, I take it we should get cracking today with whatever it is that needs to be done,' answered Isobel.

'That is correct.' said Samn. 'And, the sooner we get this sorted before the next full moon, the better the results. We need to cram these directives together as closely as possible. They are designed to complement each other.'

'Ookaayyy, the full moon, eh?' she mirrored. 'I still haven't got a clue what you are talking about. But I like to keep my word. If we are doing something that helps you today, then I am up for it.'

'We have to go back up to the Heath today. We have to clear a space,' Samn replied.

'I haven't had a single unpleasant time up on the big field with you, yet. Sounds like I can help with that. Is clearing a space like gardening?'

'Not really,' said Samn. 'What I really need is your knowledge of Hampstead Heath. I need a specific type of area for use with some of the things we bought yesterday from the voodoo shop. If I describe what kind of area I need to you, do you think you might be able to help me find somewhere suitable? If I describe an area with the type of terrain we need that's not too far from here, could you do find that for me?'

'I think so. If you give me an idea of what you are looking for in detail that would help. I know the heath well. I mean I know it well enough to get myself home whilst drunk in the dark the other day. So, try me,' she answered. Isobel let out a long, theatrical yawn.

'What we need to find is a large clearing surrounded by trees without masses of human footfall. It would be even better if it was surrounded by a few low hills or on an incline,' said Samn.

'I tell you what, let's grab the dog and hit the heath. The only way to find the perfect spot on the heath is to head out into it. I'll make some sandwiches. We can have a picnic. You pack up your bits to take with you from the voodoo shop,' said Isobel with a degree of organisation. 'Let's get to it. You know, maybe we should feed Brian first. And you know, he could do with a bath later. He's still a dog. He smells a bit funky.'

Samn smiled at Isobel. He felt that there was something refreshing about the way she could accept such unusual circumstances. He also found it strangely endearing that she looked out for Brian as though he were a real dog. Samn had known Brian for a long time and liked working with him as a partner from time to time. Brian had a chequered past. Back in the seventies, when he was a dog in his 'Son of Sam' guise, it was a plain fact to everyone involved that he had gone off on a dark tangent. He had said a lot of counterproductive things to that particular nutter in question. Samn's directors had given a very mixed response about Brian's new method of interacting with humans. He had completed the task that they asked of him, but were not pleased that he had picked a new out of the box, untested way of doing it. Some of the elders were alarmed by his choice of communication with a human. At the time, it had caused divisions within the elder group. An opposing faction felt that Brian was making some interesting new radical changes to way entities could influence humans. That faction was in approval. But most of the elders frowned upon Brian's methodologies. They felt there were too many unstable elements to it his ideas. Ultimately, they resolved to let Brian carry on. They were curious about the outcome so they treated it like an experiment. After his job was completed at the time, the directors pulled Brian back to base. After that, they rarely let him out again. It took a long to get them to trust Brian enough to allow him to oversee any further projects. Now it transpired that they were ready to risk letting him operate at least on part capacity now. Samn wasn't entirely happy that they had sent a watcher to oversee his project, but he felt relieved to see the directors now trusting Brian to get some work done again. Brian's alternative way of thinking could be an asset to Samn in a bind.

Isobel dressed in long black leggings and a fluffy, off the shoulder jumper dress. She bustled around the kitchen making sandwiches, then commenced with the task of filling up her wicker basket with napkins and cutlery. She placed a whole pack of bacon under the grill. When it was finished cooking, she used part of it to construct sandwiches and placed the rest of it on the floor on a side plate.

'Come on Brian,' she chirped. She stroked his head as he began to eat. 'Once he's finished with that we can go out.' Brian snaffled the bacon up in seconds.

With bags and baskets for lunch now packed; Samn, Isobel and Brian all headed in the direction of Hampstead Heath. It was a short walk past the terraces to get to the bridge that led them onto the lower field.

Abruptly, Brian ran off. Isobel and Samn observed as he ran around the field, sniffing at different dogs and their owners.

The two carried on walking up the hill in the direction of the less busy parts of the heath.

'So,' said Isobel, I am thinking if we go to the part of the heath that most people can't be bothered to walk to, we will find a spot where we can work without being interrupted.'

'That's perfect,' said Samn. 'As long as you

don't mind the fact that we may have to walk up there a few times to make adjustments if our work needs a bit of tweaking.'

'I like a walk on the heath, day or night,' she replied. 'And if we really don't feel like the walk, we can always take our jag to the top part and walk down to the site. It's a shorter distance. It's always good to have a second option.'

'Isn't it just?' smiled Samn.

They set off in the direction of a heavily forested section of Hampstead Heath. It was far beyond the regular paths and walkways that other locals living on the edge of the heath would visit. After taking a few wrong turns, walking into some dead ends and a few fruitless hikes up some small, heavily rooted earthen paths they finally found a suitable location. It was surrounded by a small tree path that led them to a grass-covered clearing surrounded by a bank of oak trees. A sprawling, high embankment covered in brambles and ivy flanked one side of the clearing. Isobel heard a movement in one of the bramble bushes. She went closer for inspection. A tiny rabbit scrambled into action and darted away from her in an opposite direction.

'I know it seems like a superficial question,' started Isobel, 'but will Brian find us? He's been away for quite a while and I am worried is lost on the heath.'

'Well, he found us in Soho, I wouldn't worry about him if I were you,' Samn replied. 'He's probably out looking for a new incarnation. That was another part of the conversation we had this morning.'

'Oh, well, if you like this space, let's stop for lunch and take the surroundings in for a few minutes,' she added. 'It's nice out here. This part looks like it's sheltered. Then we can do whatever you need to do after lunch.'

The two sat down by a pair of large fallen trees. Isobel started to unpack their lunch things as Samn rifled through his bag of incenses, herbs and candles. He produced 4 black candles from the bag. He stood up and began to observe the flora and fauna of the locale. He knelt and looked over some of the small plants. A great deal of the area was covered in long grass. The trees provided extra cover. Many of them were entwined with brambles and buddleia bushes.

'Ok, I think this space will work just fine,' he said to Isobel. 'Thank you for helping me find it.'

Isobel laid a small tartan blanket on the ground. Still unruffled by her present circumstances, she began laying out their sandwiches and other picnic accoutrements. After walking the perimeter of the area, Samn returned to sit beside Isobel on the blanket.

'It's quite sheltered here, is that good?' said Isobel as she handed Samn a bacon, lettuce and tomato sandwich.

Sam put it down and grabbed Isobel by the shoulders.

'I am still hungry for you,' he said.

With one sharp yank, he pulled her clothes from her shoulders exposing her breasts. She could felt the chilled air on her body. It excited her. Samn grabbed both of her breasts. He began sucking her nipples and gently biting her flesh. He ran his tongue along the entire length of her neck and bit the side of her cheek before plunging his tongue deeply inside of her mouth, whilst he continued to pinch and grab at her breasts lustfully.

Isobel could feel herself getting wet again. There was something exciting about fucking in the woods. Isobel always felt aroused by it. It was more than just the freezing air, there was something very primal about sex outside. It gave her a sense of being more in touch with the animal part of her as all sense of ceremony seemed to fade away. She made a mental note to herself to spend more time fucking in woodland areas in future.

Samn grabbed her by her hair and pulled her head back. She loved the way that felt. He began to suck and bite at her neck and earlobes. She could feel the spot where he had been licking her breasts and neck get colder. She felt her pink nipples get rock hard as he sucked on them.

Momentarily, Samn stopped and looked up across the clearing. In a far corner of the forest, he spied the figure of a middle-aged man watching them through the trees. If he was correct in his estimation, the man was wanking himself off.

Samn smiled and turned back to Isobel.

'I think we are being observed,' he said.

'By who?' said Isobel, soundly slightly alarmed.

'Just some random stranger,' he whispered, kissing her cheek. He pushed her clothes down more, exposing her torso and stomach. 'I think we should give him a show. I don't think he knows that I have spotted him,' said Samn.

Isobel kissed Samn. She turned her body inwards towards him. It made her feel more protected from whoever was out there, but she still liked this new that idea he had come up with. She sat up, to completely remove her fluffy sweater. Samn stuck his hand down the front of her leggings and grabbed her pussy. He could feel how wet she was. He kissed her again. She reached over and felt between his legs at the bulge that was straining to be let loose. The feeling was delicious.

Samn stopped and quickly spied out into the woods

again.

'That guy is intently watching us and wanking. And if I am correct, there is a younger guy watching us as well about thirty feet away from him.'

Isobel tried to stifle a giggle.

'Damned heath, you can't get no privacy round here no matter where you go. Who would have guessed?'

'Well, if we need to come back here it will be mostly at night anyway,' he answered.

'I don't care. We're never going to see them again. Who cares?' she smiled.

Samn hiked Isobel's leggings and knickers down around her ankles and spread her legs. With two fingers, he started to finger fuck and slap her pussy. Isobel gasped. She could feel the freezing air, mixed with the sharp, painful pleasures of his slapping begin to rouse her. She writhed as the excitement took her over. The sensation was heightened more so by the fact that she knew her naked breasts and pussy were exposed, and that this spectacle was being observed by two complete strangers. She thought about them at the edges of the woods, watching and playing with themselves. If she orchestrated it right, she thought, she may well be able to make several people cum at once. The thought was a massive turn on. Samn leant over her stomach and put his face fully inside of her pussy. He started to lick her. Isobel stared into the blue sky. She noticed one of the men quietly edge his way out of the woods and sidle up towards them in a very precocious fashion. He was still clutching his erection. Isobel looked at him and gave him a half-smile. The man, now more confident in the belief that it was okay for him to approach, walked closer to the perimeter of Samn and Isobel. He stood out of the way and stared, transfixed, as Samn carried on licking Isobel's wet pussy. Isobel toyed with the idea in her mind of what it might feel like to have the cock of a stranger in her mouth. He wasn't a bad looking guy. To her, he was average, but not ugly or scary.

She knew already if she wanted it, she could easily have it. After a few minutes, the second man approached and started watching them. He carried on wanking from a few feet away. Sam held her down by her wrists and began fucking her. Isobel's eyes rolled into the back of her head. Her mind became fixated on thinking about all the cocks that were surrounding her and how many of them she could fit inside of her all at once. She wasn't sure if she would go ahead with implementing that idea, but she certainly liked thinking about it. She looked at Samn, considering the idea.

He turned her around and knelt her onto all fours and began to fuck her from behind. She could see the two men watching openly nearby. She could see that they were becoming more aroused by her moans and yelps.

The average-looking man walked over to the blanket. He seemed to be gleaning something from Isobel's eyes, looking for approval. She was so lost in the way the forceful way Samn was fucking her, that caught herself nodding a 'yes' to him. He crouched down and grabbed one of her breasts as it shook from the force of Samn ploughing her from behind. The feeling of a stranger touching her made her even more horny. It had an effect that reinforced her inner animal desires. In this moment, there was no need for formality or negotiations. There was also no need to try and explain why they should all be doing this, because everyone was having fun. It really didn't matter. It was the fulfilment of needs and desires. She felt part of a strange animal act based entirely on pure supply and demand. It was sexual minimalism in its greatest sense. Isobel grabbed the stranger's cock and put it in her mouth. From behind her, Samn caught one look at what she had done with the stranger. She could feel him getting harder inside of her. The second guy approached her. He stood staring, watching and wanking over the scene.

Isobel savoured the taste of a strange cock in her mouth. The fascination wasn't so much as to how his cock tasted, as much as the surreal feeling of how it made her mind feel. She didn't feel unsafe surrounded by the strangers. She knew exactly why they were there, what their agenda was, and because they were quite polite and respectful about it, it made it okay to play. She was just relieved Samn wasn't offended by her spontaneous decision to suck a stranger's cock.

Isobel continued with a series of muffled moans and grunts as she watched the guy wanking, she could see his cum was building and his face became full of concentration as he stood over her staring straight at her mouth. Her cunt began to flood again. She could feel herself about to cum. Samn grabbed her by the neck and momentarily cut off her air supply, she wasn't sure if he had done it on purpose but she didn't want him to stop. There was something about this moment of oxygen starvation. It caused another massive orgasm to begin to build up. She let out a scream that she surprised herself with, as she came. She felt a little bit guilty for being so noisy about it. A few seconds later the stranger came and moaned loudly as Samn pumped her pussy with an increasing violence.

Her took his cock out of her cunt and groaned. He moved towards her face.

'Open your eyes,' he demanded.

Isobel held her eyes open and watched as Samn strained to cum over her face. She felt a spurt of spunk fall directly into her left eye. Samn wailed with rapture and collapsed onto the blanket beside her. The two men, not knowing what to do, stood to one side, as though waiting for instruction.

'The show is over, boys,' said Samn. 'Hit the road.' Isobel smiled and found a tissue to use to rub the spunk out of her eyes. She let out a little laugh.

coupled with a slight cough to correct her breathing.

The form of a bristled black dog with fiery red eyes appeared beside Samn and Isobel. He barked fiercely at the two men and growled viciously. Both men, now alarmed, disappeared back into the woods. Once the dog's hackles were down they realised it was only Brian. Isobel and Samn still felt a bit spaced out from their respective orgasms. Brian left their side and began to walk around the perimeter of the clearing, sniffing and letting out a few short barks as though to ward off any other people who may be in the thicket. He returned and settled on a patch of long grass nearby. Brian gave Samn a soulful look. Samn could feel a little look of approval about the space they had found. His red eyes sparkled. Brian started to pant. It made him look like as though he was smiling.

'You know Brian,' said Samn. 'The concept of you in this guise, might be a clever idea after all.'

Chapter 6 The Rite

Samn and Isobel got up and began to rearrange their clothing. Isobel unwrapped a sandwich and bit into it. She took the other half of the sandwich and gave it to Brian. He snaffled it up.

'Thanks Brian, for scaring them off. That helped us disperse any post orgasmic formalities. All that action made me hungry,' said Isobel. Her cheeks were still flushed.

Samn unwrapped a sandwich and poured out some coffee from their flask. He took a sip from the metal cup and passed it over to Isobel.

'Ta, after this we can make a start,' she said.

'Of course,' he replied. 'Although, what we just did was already the beginning of the rite we need to carry out. I hadn't planned it that way. But it just occurred to me part way through, that this would definitely help give it a big push.'

'Well that's good then, I don't think you will catch me complaining about it,' said Isobel. 'Just show me what we need to do and let's get it done.'

After their food was finished, Isobel packed their things away back into the basket.
Samn handed two of the black candles to Isobel and

held on to the other two himself. He started to give Isobel her directions.

'Okay, what I need you for you to do is help me build four corners. They need to be as close to the edge of the woods in this clearing as you can manage. I will take this end and you take the opposite side. If we stand facing opposite each other we can accurately gauge the distance. We need to try and make the square as equal as possible. It's not an exact science but it shouldn't be too difficult. Try and find the most sheltered spot you can, so the candle won't go out. If it blows out when relight it, but try and get somewhere out of the breeze,' Isobel nodded at him enthusiastically, registering that she understood.

The two paced away from each other in opposite directions slowly, as if they were about to fight a duel. After choosing a spot that looked like a good place for the first candle, Isobel turned around and looked over her shoulder to see if Samn agreed with her about the choice of her location. He nodded and shouted, 'That's good, Yes!'

Then turning left, the both walked slowly across opposite ends of the clearing and placed the second lot of candles in the far corners of the field. Isobel put one candle down. It didn't look quite right. She picked it up and placed it back down in a slightly further spot. She decided that it now looked more correct. She turned and looked over at Samn. He nodded and shouted towards her, 'That's perfect just there!'

She walked back to the picnic blanket and waited expectantly for the next directive. Samn produced two bags of black coloured powder and some herbs and handed one of the bags to her.

'Now, you need to poke a small hole in the corner of the bag and let it carefully run out. We need to link all the candles together. Be careful not to let it all run out in one place. I have a little more of this black salt in my bag, but it will save us having to go back to the flat to get more if we do this right the first time.

'Okay,' said Isobel.

Isobel ripped a small corner in the base of the bag and watched as a tiny amount of the grains of black powder fell to the ground. She decided to make the hole in the bag slightly larger to ensure that the coverage was spread evenly over the ground.

'Damn,' said Samn. 'I made the hole in the bag too big.' He grabbed the base of the plastic bag and tried to stem the flow of black sand. 'It's okay. I brought more, so we *will* get this right on the first go. I am sure of it.'

Carefully, they paced across opposite ends of the clearing. They carefully spread the black sand in the straightest lines they could manage between the black candles. Samn returned to the satchel of provisions that were placed beside the picnic blanket. He fished out the second bag of black powder. He continued to spread it from his corner of the square towards Isobel's section of the field.

'Okay,' he said. 'That looks pretty good.'

'I don't really know what we are doing,' said Isobel. 'But in truth, I don't mind that much, as long as it helps you. If we are being productive, I am happy to assist.'

'Oh, it's helping,' said Samn with some resolve. 'It will be a very pretty spectacle in a few minutes, as well. You'll like it. Now, come back to the blanket. We need to copy this sigil out onto the paper four times.'

Sam fished around his bag. He presented Isobel with one of a pair of black pens and some parchment paper he had procured from the voodoo shop. He drew something out on one of them and handed it to her. It was a circular symbol with a cross through it. It each corner of the circle a different symbol had been drawn inside of it. They were spidery looking and unfamiliar to her. Underneath the circle, he had drawn a picture of spear with a heart on the end of the tip. He put an x through the centre of the spear and handed it to Isobel.

'Copy this out twice, then show it to me,' instructed Samn.

Isobel took the parchment paper and the pen from his hand. She set about copying the symbols by using an example that he had set down next to her. He carried on drawing a second image of the print himself. Isobel handed the drawing back to Samn. He checked them over.

'That looks okay, but if it hadn't been okay we have enough paper here to do it a second time. But these look okay. They don't have to be perfect, just similar. Now what we do is place each piece of paper under each of the black candles at the corners. You do your two corners and I will do my two corners,' Samn directed.

Isobel complied. It was kind of fun taking part in a ritual without really knowing the exact outcome. It felt slightly mischievous but it also had an exhilarating air about it. Outside of this setting, Isobel felt that anyone else may have taken her actions to seem reckless, but Isobel wasn't much in the habit of caring about other people's views. The entire world was reckless, as far as she was concerned. At least this was prescribed recklessness. It was interesting how her inner voice felt like sometimes it could be made up of a thousand conversations she had had with various people over the decades, and yet she was still inclined to follow her own beliefs. It could feel very rebellious to ignore her conscience at times like this. On top of that, she liked having Samn and Brian around. They were so fresh and new. She enjoyed their company.

Samn returned to the blanket and produced something from his jacket. It was vial of green liquid contained in an ornate glass bottle with a silver top. There were markings etched on the glass that had similar markings resembling the symbols. The silver top was cast in the shape of creature. It looked like an archaic version of a grimacing dog. He linked arms with Isobel.

'For this part, we must walk in a circle, going counter-clockwise,' said Samn.

'What's in the bottle?' she quizzed.

'Something that was presented to me. Let's just say it belongs to a couple of friends who have been playing chess for a very long time.'

Isobel looked at him with a raised eyebrow and a half frown.

'I have no idea what you are talking about,' stated Isobel.

'We'll get there, don't worry,' he said with a comforting tone. 'Bear with me. You'll understand what I mean so enough.'

The two paced slowly around the circle, drops from the bottle splashed onto the ground. It linked up the four corners. Isobel had to admit, this was kind of fun. It felt a lot like following a recipe without knowing what it was going to make.

They paced around the full length of the square, sprinkling liquid from the ornate bottle as they went.

When their walk was completed, Samn lit a cigarette. He offered one to Isobel and she accepted.

'Now, stand back you two,' he said firmly to Isobel and Brian. They each took several paces backwards. Isobel was curious about what was going to happen next.

Samn knelt to beside the point where the liquid had been first spilled. He set it alight.

A tiny, thin line of fire began to glow all the way around the perimeter. The four candles burst into flames along with the parchment underneath it. An erratic red glow began to rise and coil from within the circle. It was beautiful. Tiny firework-like explosions mixed with dancing rings of light began to emit from the ground. It reminded Isobel of aurora borealis. She looked up into the trees. The wind rushed violently over the canopy of the forest. She could hear a faint sound of whispering voices, and saw dark shadowy figures dart between the trees and bushes. She couldn't quite catch sight of them nor could she hear exactly what was being said by them. They were one step ahead of her peripheral vision, but she knew something was out there.

Samn and Brian stood frozen, listening.

'I think that's a good sign,' said Samn calmly.

'Is it?' said Isobel tentatively.

'Yes, if I am right in thinking. That's the rite done. Well, the first rite, anyway. We can go back to the flat now.'

Isobel pointed to the glowing circle. 'Will it stay like that? What is that?'

'It's a portal my dear. The glowing and the whispering will stay around for a while, but not enough to draw attention to itself out here. All we have to do now is go home and see if it takes hold or not.'

'Is it a bit like the tree?'

'Yeah,' he replied.

Samn grabbed her by the hand and began to walk back down across the heath with her. Brian stayed behind, sniffing around the clearing. He then soon caught up with them.

'I think he's "watching",' said Isobel.

The daylight was starting to fade. In November, it could get dark very quickly at that time of the year. They quickened their pace.

Isobel lit up another cigarette for herself and walked along the woodland path beside Samn thoughtfully, as they headed back home. She felt displaced in her feelings about what had just happened. In fact, she wasn't exactly sure what had just happened. She liked this new sense of the unknown happening. To act, without knowing the outcome felt very liberating to her mind. She turned to Samn.

'If you came from a tree, and that portal back there is a new type of door, then where did Brian come from?' she asked curiously.

'I expect he came from a pub in Soho,' said Samn. 'There's a bar over there that a Mr. Crowley used to drink in. They used to let him use the cellar for his various machinations and rituals. Brian probably used that entryway. I mean, I am making an educated guess. I will ask him later to see what he says. It's probably that though. A lot of the portals Crowley laid down around Soho are still active and usable. He was good like that. He was way ahead of his time.'

'I have heard of him, but I didn't know that,' replied Isobel.

The two walked over the heath passing Parliament Hill once again. They strode over the bridge and quietly passed the large terraced houses until they reached the front door of their little flat.

'What shall we do now, while we are waiting?'

said Samn expectantly.

'I'd quite like to give Brian a bath,' said Isobel. Perhaps she was too distracted by events, but she had failed to pick up on his seductive overtures.

Samn huffed, 'Okay then,' he said.

'If you feel like it later, we could cook something,' she added.

Isobel busied herself in the bathroom stripping out the extraneous cleaning products that were placed around the edge of the bath in an attempt to make way for the dog. Samn walked into the bedroom. He plonked down onto the bed. He could feel how the ritual had drained a lot of energy from him, but he didn't see much point in complaining to Isobel about it. The reason he had been given this new energy in the first place was to carry out the directives his administrators had requested of him. He stared out of the window with silent resolve. He wanted to try and recharge his batteries as quickly as possible, so he could back to enjoying his new guise. He listened to Isobel, who was clanking around in the bathroom whilst running the bath water. He could hear her chatting to Brian in a chirpy voice as though he were a real dog. He then heard her singing to him to calm him down as she oversaw his dog bath.

'Good doggy!' he heard Isobel exclaim. That was the last sound that drifted through his ears as he fell into a deep sleep. He was starting to recall the sensation of constriction that human weariness could cause. It had been a long time since he had felt like that. He chuckled at the way Isobel treated Brian. No matter what Brian really was, Samn got the impression that, to Isobel, Brian was mainly just a cute, fluffy dog. He found that level of innocence about her quite attractive. Then, with eyelids feeling too heavy, he let them close.

Samn found himself walking along a small, quiet cobbled street in the centre of the banking district of the City of London. It was a very old district, with its' own police force, different powers to the rest of London and very small residential population of about fourteen thousand people. The square mile of London always felt different from the rest of the city. There wasn't a lot there. It was a very suited and booted area made up mostly of modern bars, endless offices and forgettable sandwich shops. A mixture of Georgian buildings flanked by glass monolithic skyscrapers lined his way as he walked along the city street. He spied a tiny cellar bar and felt compelled to go down the pokey cement staircase. He faced the tiny wooden door that led to the entrance. A black metal sign above the door read "The Wine Library" in faded gold script. The sign looked like it hadn't been repainted in decades. Samn had to duck down to get through the pokey little doorway. As he entered the bar, a few customers turned around to look at him momentarily, then turned back to their drinks. A long bar bedecked with glass shelves and glittering bottles filled the length of one side. He looked at the chalk board behind the bar and began to read it. The bartender resembled the one he had seen in Camden the night before. The bartender slid up to Samn, and cut him off before he could place an order.

'I have a present for you. It's compliments of the house,' he said enigmatically.

The bartender presented Samn with a large square casket that resembled a treasure chest. It was filled up with pink grapefruit coloured alcohol and a great deal of ice. The bartender placed a roman candle at each corner of the box. As he lit them, swirling fireworks and lights resembling the ones from the heath began to rise from the sparklers. The bartender pushed the large chest filled with alcohol towards Samn and motioned for him to pick it up. Samn complied. He was surprised by weight of this unfeasibly large cocktail casket as he attempted to carry it away from the bar. The bartender opened a tiny blue cocktail umbrella and balanced it inside of a paper straw. He added it to the edge of the casket.

'There you go, all set!' he said enthusiastically.

'Thanks,' said Samn, looking over the spectacular cocktail with confused wonder.

Samn stopped to survey the room momentarily. The oak wood panelling and multitude of shelves loaded with old books and curios made the room seem very stately. The tables and chairs were had very careworn and antiquated. The room looked like it had not changed in centuries. One wall was lined entirely with faded, dusty hardbound books. The spines had deteriorated on a few of the volumes. Each table had a large black candelabra festooned with lighted white candles placed in the centre. At the far end of the long bar Samn could see several cubby holes and alcoves. Light glowed from the tables set back from the main bar in the little rooms. He poked his head through each alcove to see if there were any tables free. But most of the tables were occupied. There was a strange mix of people in the rooms, some of them were in very expensive looking suits, whilst others at the tables were dressed in formal military attire. The clothing looked like it was from a different era to now. He passed by a slick looking black girl. She winked at him. She was speaking to one man in a language that sounded like Russian, but he couldn't be sure. In another alcove, one girl was dressed in full Brazilian carnival wear as she chatted to a group of dark figures cloaked entirely in black. They had covered their faces in a variety of horse, rabbit, and sheep masks. This bar was very proving to be very peculiar.

'I wonder if this a costume party?' he thought to himself. It was hard to understand what the occasion was. Everything felt very hazy.

He spied the entrance to a back room and decided that it might be propitious to seek a table there. His large cocktail was starting to feel heavy. As he approached the passageway that led to the backroom, he could hear laughter, yelps and whipping noises.

Samn walked past the busy alcoves headed for the back room. As people at the tables continued talking and chatting; a long, black patent leather laced up boot embellished with 10 inch spiked heels darted out from under one of the tables and rested between his legs, holding him in place. He stopped and peered into the candlelit alcove. A beautiful woman in her early 30's stared up at him from the table with a cheeky smile. She had long black hair styled into a bouffant. Her eyes were framed by heavy, retro-looking black eyelashes. She was wearing a black leather bra and a matching pencil skirt. This was covered by a full-length fishnet dress, finished off with a spiked black leather choker. Her legs were covered in black lace stockings and suspenders. A pair of zip-up black patent leather gloves covered her arms to the top of her armpit. Four sharp spikes protruded from the knuckles of each glove. She clenched her fist.

'You don't want to go back there,' she said playfully, in a soft Scottish accent. 'It's like purgatory back there. Once you get in, you never get out. Besides, all the tables are full. Come and sit with us.' The woman scooted over along the bench in her alcove. She patted the seat beside her, and motioned for Samn to sit down.

An incredibly elegant looking older man sat beside her in the alcove. His hair was trained back into a long braid that nearly touched his waist. He struck a match, and lit a few of the candles on their tables' candelabra. The light began to illuminate their faces.

There was something very Edwardian in the look of this man. He had trained his dark moustache and beard to sharp points. His beautifully cut dark green tweed suit and off-white linen shirt seemed to look more Edwardian than modern. His short, black leather gloves were decorated with gold rings. Many of them were in the shape of crowned animal skulls. The eyes of each skull sparkled with glistening jewels. One of his hands rested on the table clutching a gold pocket watch. It gave off an inordinately loud ticking noise that permeated the tiny alcove.

The table was overladen with empty drinks glasses. A backgammon board was set on one corner, the game looked as though it was in play. It was situated in a juxtaposition between the couple.

'Come, sit down, join us,' said the beautiful woman with a welcoming tone. 'You can put your drink down here.' With an overzealous sweeping motion using her patent gloved arm, she cleared the table of all the empty glasses in one fell swoop. They crashed indiscreetly onto the floor, spilling out into the aisle beside the alcove. Samn turned back to the bar to survey what the bartender's reaction might be, but he seemed to be paying the matter no attention.

'It's okay,' she said, abating his fears. 'Sit

down! This is my bar and these are my glasses. I can do what I like with them.' The woman shot Samn a naughty smile.

Samn set the huge cocktail chest down on the table. He sat down beside the beautiful woman and looked at the couple, still feeling slightly dazed. He watched as the last Roman candle fizzled out in the box.

He couldn't help but feel the enormous pull of her sexuality pervading through him. It was so overwhelming that he felt intoxicated by it. Not only was she visually beautiful, but she seemed to have an aura around her that pulled him towards her like a powerful tractor beam. He leaned over to the cocktail chest and sucked a large gulp of the alcohol out of the box, trying steady himself.

'I am glad you stopped by,' she said calmly. 'I was just flirting with my colleague here, but you'll prove to make a useful temporary distraction before he manages to get the upper hand.'

The man smiled and shifted in his seat making himself more comfortable. He crossed his legs and folded his hands, letting them rest on the table.

'You could have supplied some more comfortable cushions for these seats, my dear,' he said jovially. 'I am going to have to get very drunk to not notice how hard these benches are.'

'How hard what is? Is something's hard I definitely want to know about it.' she teased at him.

He let out a little laugh.

The woman extended her gloved hand and ran it along the man's thigh. She put her glove out behind her and stroked Samn's thigh at the same time. Samn felt his cock become instantly hard by her actions. Her masterful touch surged through him like a jolt of electricity. He swallowed hard to stop himself from losing his self-control. He took another huge gulp of his drink using the straw, as it was the only coping mechanism available to him at that moment. He could feel the alcohol beginning to take effect.

'Please don't do that again, I feel like I am out of my depth with you,' croaked Samn feebly.

'Not at all! Not at all!' said the man in a conciliatory manner, 'You were invited! We wanted to talk to you. We want to see how you are doing.'

Samn screwed up in face. This alcohol had hit him quickly, and in the worst way. He noticed he was grabbing the edge of the table to stay upright. He stared up into the ceiling trying to find some point in the room that didn't make him feel dizzy. His eyes rested on a small group of party-goers and suited men slam dancing in the corner to the most amazing rap-style heavy metal. The unusual looking display of slam dancers laughed as they jumped and crashed into each other. A carnival-clad Brazilian woman was performing a striptease at the edge of the crowd. She was grinding her ass lasciviously into the face of a four-foot-tall man who was dressed up as a mediaeval jester.

Samn swirled his drunken gaze back to the direction of the woman and the man at his table.
He rubbed the palm of his hand over his forehead and pawed it down across his face. He realised he was now fully drunk, and beyond the point of return.

'I am sorry, that drink... I think I'm pissed,' he announced helplessly to the couple.

The woman lifted a tiny black leather spiked purse from her lap. She produced a bottle of pills and showed it to him. Opening the bottle, she shook the pills out over the backgammon board. The woman picked up one and popped it into the gaping mouth of the man beside her. She then took several herself from the table and swallowed them all in one go. She lifted another tablet and framed it with her index finger and thumb, facing Samn.

'Here, have one of these. It will help,' she said confidently.

'I ... err. I don't know if I should,' he garbled.

The woman grabbed one his shoulders to steady him. 'It will be okay, I promise,' she said.

Again, the point of contact where she touched his shoulder made him feel punch drunk. Her touch had an unearthly power to it. He felt his mouth open involuntarily in shock. The beautiful woman deposited the pill onto his tongue and used the flat of her gloved hand to shut his gaping jaws. She motioned towards his drink and he took another sip. Samn swallowed the mysterious pill.

The pill took effect very quickly, and it was by far the most interesting drug he had ever experienced. From the moment he had swallowed it, it felt like a tiny glowing golden beam of light was tracing a line from the tip of his tongue to the base of his stomach. In his mind's eye, he could see the gold beam pulsing through his whole body.

He felt strange as the pill worked its' way into the pit of his stomach at an alarming speed. At first, he felt a tickling in the base of his loins, followed by a feeling that could only be described as a type of orgasmic pleasure. It shot up through the length of his torso like a spacecraft that had exploded into a thousand fragments. He could feel each individual blood cell detonate into a wave of distilled bliss, as his eyes hurtled towards the centre of the sun. He grabbed the edge of his seat and convulsed with the most violent of raptures.

The man and the woman looked on with interest. They had clearly not been as affected by their dose of the drug as he was, but they were still intent on witnessing the way it was affecting him with a degree of amusement.

The beautiful woman sighed and turned to her counterpart.

'Let's give him a minute,' she said to the man. 'He will settle down in a little while.'

Samn felt a raging tsunami of pure pleasure rocketing through the very fabric of his being. It electrified every nerve and brain cell. His brain felt like it was being taken apart like a set of toy plastic bricks, then being rearranged again. He now felt like a highly-tuned engine. Stars formed on the lenses of his eyes. The front and back of his mind began to swap places. He almost lost consciousness as an orgasm raced through the length of his spine. He stifled an unintended yowl of uncontrollable ecstasy.

The woman watched in a nonplussed manner. She calmly peeled a large Cuban cigar with her thumbs and began to heat it up with a flame from a candle.

'You know,' she said churlishly, 'when you have an orgasm like that; it is said that that is the closest thing you will ever experience to seeing the face of God.'

Samn collapsed on the floor. With Samn still lolling in his stupor, the man politely picked him up, dusted him off ceremoniously and settled him back on his chair.

'Are you okay, now?' said the man politely.

'Uh yeah, I think so,' replied Samn. 'I think I can see through time.' He gazed at the man's eyes. In Samn's peripheral vision, a small spotted iguana scuttled up the man's suit. It disappeared over his shoulder. Samn swayed slightly to the left to try to see where that iguana went, but it was to no avail.

'Did that pill help a bit?' the man asked Samn.

Sam looked through him, but his mind was now completely in subspace.

'I, I, err, yeah.' Samn answered in a half-aware, discombobulated tone.

The man reached over to pat him on the shoulder.

'You're all right,' We did say you would be, and you are.' He let out another little signature chuckle. 'We're only playing, only playing, nothing serious. Don't worry.' said the Edwardian-looking man.

'Hmm,' said the woman. 'That was fun.' She fished another pill out from her bag and popped another one into her mouth. I wish these things had *that* effect on me. These days they don't. However, it's nice to watch someone else enjoying the full force of them. When that happens, I can sometimes still feel a little memory of that first rapture still tickling inside of me, but that was a long time ago,' she said with a sigh. 'Still, it's nice to watch the raw effects.'

'You have to make your own fun,' replied the elegant man to the beautiful woman.
The beautiful woman spied the man with a slightly lustful raised eyebrow. She knelt up onto the long bench at the back of the booth.

'Indeed, you do. Let's just leave the subject of Samn to one side for a moment whilst he recovers. He looks like he could use a little time to himself.'

Hiking her spiked heels at a 45-degree angle, she began to crawl on her leather-gloved hands and black-stockinged knees across the bench to where the man was sitting. She straddled the full weight of her body across his lap, spreading a knee either side of his thighs. Lewdly, she started to softly grind her pussy into his lap.

'Now, where were we?' she said smiling.

'I think we were talking about dark matter,' he replied. He squirmed in his seat with the obvious frustration the beautiful woman was currently causing him. She could hear his voice quiver under his cool demeanour. Her black glossy lips curled into a licking smile as she felt his groin beneath her swell.

The man grabbed her fishnet dress and ripped the front open. He produced a switchblade from his jacket and cut the centre of her leather bra in two. With both leather gloves extended he began to knead her rounded white breasts and hard red nipples as she hovered above him, straddling his lap. She knew that grinding in his lap would be quite maddening to him. She sank her tongue into his mouth and kissed him hungrily whilst pulling his head back by his long plait. He grabbed her head and turned it to one side as he began to lick the length of her neck. He motioned for her to stand up. She balanced effortlessly on her high spiked heels. The man loomed over her. He was almost twice her height. She bent over the bench and grabbed a piece of panelling in the corner of the alcove. Samn watched in amazement as a huge, grizzled looking indeterminately-shaped animal cock rose out of the man's trousers as he removed his clothes. His hips and thighs were covered with a thick, dark, flowing hair like that of a goat. Samn looked down at the floor. His feet were a pair of large hooves resembling that of a large goat.

The beautiful woman looked over her shoulder and smiled at him with a glow of delight.

The older man straightened his cock and rubbed it a few times as he stared at the woman smiling at him from over her shoulder. With a single movement of his tongue bearing down upon he small of her back, he licked her harshly until he reached the nape of her neck.

Grabbing her roughly by the shoulders with a single, unearthly groan, he simultaneously sank his teeth into the nape of her neck as he forced the entire length of his animal-like prick into the deepest reaches of her ass.

The woman gasped sharply and let out a deviant laugh.

'You always know how to push my buttons,' she hissed.

Samn watched the spectacle. He was mesmerised by the half-human, half-demonic looking figure as he pillaged the beautiful woman's ass with ferocious hunger. He found it impossible to look away. A crowd began to gather around the table and watch the show as the table and chairs in the alcove began to shake under the pressure. The man stopped and repositioned himself. He pulled both of her arms behind her back and proceeded to plunge his hard cock into the beautiful woman's cunt. Books and bottles fell from the shelves. The dancers in the corner stopped abruptly with the same degree of alertness that would precede the threat of a natural disaster. One or two stayed adamantly beside the table to watch, but others began to file out of the bar. It was as if they knew something that Samn didn't.

Samn sat captive, unable to move from his bewildered glaze as people from the bar began to make a hurried exit. They darted out of the front door like sand falling through an hourglass. Arms and legs crushed their way up the stairs to the exit that led to the street. People shouted and whooped excitedly as they dashed away, their voices faded towards unknown places in the night. The devil man grunted. He continued to fuck the leather-clad girl with his gargantuan cock. She let out an unworldly, low banshee-like howl. It shook the very foundations of the bar into an earthquake.

Samn was deafened by the man's decibel roar as debris-filled wind whipped through the room. Hail resembling ice bolts and small fireballs careened through the air in the bar, setting alight any object where the hurtling embers could find purchase. Samn watched helplessly as the room became engulfed in a twisted spiral of bellowing flames. He knew that shortly, by the way the two were howling and roaring, that either one or both were close to orgasm. Black creature-shaped shadows danced amidst the inferno to the tune of an ear-shattering climax from the devil man. Samn covered his ears and began to scream.

Samn woke up.

Samn snapped awake and shook himself out of the bedsheets in shock. Still feeling shaken by the dream, he sat up and looked out the window to see the pinks and purples of the dawn sky rising over London.

He looked down at the side of the bed and noticed Brian was fast asleep on a pile of luxuriant damp-looking towels. He could hear the faint tapping of computer keys in the living room.

'Hello?' called Samn from bedroom. He listened as Isobel pushed the chair back at her desk. She got up to and walked through to the bedroom.

She was wearing a long, black fishnet dress identical to the one the beautiful woman had been wearing in the bar. Strangely, she jumped on the bed and straddled Samn's legs in the exact same manner as the woman had to the devil man in the bar. Samn felt a bit spooked by it, but said nothing.

Teasingly, she began to grind into Samn's lap playfully as the sleepy dog on the towels below let out a high-pitched yawn.

'You slept for 12 hours!' she said excitedly. 'I guess you were really tired!'

'I guess I was,' said Samn. There was a mumbling tone of half-asleep confusion still in his voice.

'Do you feel better after your sleep?' chirped Isobel. 'That dog is nice and clean now.'

Samn smiled a little. Only someone like Isobel would be pragmatic enough to decide that a dark creature like Brian would still need a bath.

Isobel looked down at the twisted bedclothes. A

gleaming silver knife edged with a shining black handle and engraved with illegible gold script lay precariously at the edge of the bed. It was just on the cusp of falling down the back of the bed. She picked it up and examined it.

'Hmm,' she said quizzically. 'Is this yours?'

Samn stared at the unfamiliar dagger. It glinted as he looked at it. A tiny puff of fire shot from the tip of the blade. Isobel promptly dropped the knife back onto the bed and jumped with a miniature jolt of fright.

'I guess it's mine now, yeah,' said Samn. 'And I think that means we have yet another busy day ahead of us.'

Chapter 7 The Knife

Samn lifted the dagger as it nestled between the bedclothes and examined it more closely. He flipped over the blade to examine the script that was written on the other side. Turning the knife over, he felt certain that the script on the blade had changed.

Isobel, a little bit unnerved by the strange implement, decided to head into the kitchen. She began to prepare everyone's breakfast. Samn could hear her humming and singing to herself as she slammed refrigerator doors and busied herself with clanging pans. He heard her wrangling with lighting the ignition on the stove.

Brian the dog sat up and looked at Samn expectantly. He jumped up onto the bed and staring into Samn's eyes, then ran a single paw over Samn's face. Samn patted Brian on the head and pushed him to the bottom of the bed with his leg. He wanted to try to figure out what was this new knife was all about. He stared at the strange object curiously.

The characters and engraving on the spine started to shift and change of its own accord. He flipped the knife over once again to see what was written on the other side. The words 'Hi Samn!' appeared along the spine of the blade. Samn stared at the knife, amazed.

'Guess who this is?' next appeared written on the knife's spine. 'I will give you two guesses.'

Brian lifted his head from the bedsheets and let out a suspicious 'Wuff.'

'Is it who I think it is from last night?' he asked the knife inquisitively.

'No,' wrote out the knife across its' spine. 'It's that handsome devil you met last night. Once "Madame" executes any new directives, she doesn't like to get involved with the details. She leaves that up to me in this capacity.' The knife shifted again. 'She doesn't like to be seen to be micromanaging a situation. I however, disagree with her methods. I like to be available to offer help and guidance. But it's something we have had to agree to disagree on, for a very long time.'

'Oh well, I can understand both viewpoints,' said Samn quietly, to the knife.

'Who are you speaking to?' called Isobel through from the kitchen. Samn looked up and saw through the narrow passageway a snippet of Isobel as she battled with a pair of mewing kittens. They were busy rubbing and tumbling around her legs as she tried to quickly spoon their kitten food out into two separate dishes from a large tin.

'I will tell you over breakfast,' he hollered

back towards the direction of the passageway.

Samn looked back down at the knife.

'Madame decided this knife would be novel form of communication to help you on your way to your next directive. We need you again today. There's really not a great deal of time to spare. You will need to get your skates on.'

'I am still exhausted from yesterday. I feel like I haven't slept at all.'

'Well, never mind,' answered the knife, 'You might catch a little more sleep later this evening after you have gone out and attended to our next ordinance. Today you will be heading to Westminster. You need to be near Big Ben and the Houses of Parliament. It's a very striking location. We are both very pleased with the site for our latest endeavour.

'The location for what endeavour?' replied Samn.

'Why the new portal of course,' responded the script on the knife.

Samn shook his head.

'Of course, I knew there was to be more than one portal, but I was not aware that it was going to be in such a conspicuous location. Had I known that I may not have agreed to this particular job. This might be difficult.'

'There's nothing conspicuous about where you are going. That place is swarmed every day with a variety of tourists and protesters from all corners of the earth. No one is going to bat an eyelid about what you get up to. Chill out.'

Isobel called for Brian from the kitchen. She had placed two fully-constructed cheeseburgers on a plate on the floor for him. She opened a small packet of bacon fries and scattered them over the plate for the dog. He walked towards the food and began to snaffle it up.

'I really will have to think about getting him some proper dog chow. This is not responsible. A dog needs proper nutrition,' Isobel whispered under her breath.

She lifted a tray and carried it through to the bedroom. On the tray were two plates of bacon and eggs, a pot of tea and a small side plate comprising of miniature buttered bagels. She sat down beside Sam and began to place the dishes on the bedside table.

'I will be back in a minute with cups, cutlery and milk,' she said cheerfully.

Isobel walked back in the direction of the kitchen.

The knife printed out another message to Samn.

'Take the knife with you today. We will make sure you complete your task if you have it with you. It will be easy. I promise.'

Samn placed both hands over his face and yawned. 'Okay. But if I do get the opportunity to acquire some uninterrupted sleep at some point today, I would certainly appreciate it.'

'Done,' printed the knife.

Isobel returned from the kitchen carrying two mugs and two sets of knives and forks. She was also holding a little jug of milk. She placed it all on the bedside table.

'Four minutes. It takes four minutes to let the tea steep properly and here is your fork. I wasn't sure if you needed a knife or were planning on using the one in the bed,' she said with a cheeky grin.

'We have to go to Parliament Square today,' said Samn with a slightly exasperated tone.

'Well I guess dogging is off the menu then,' replied Isobel with a titter. 'That's okay, I'll ravish you later. You know Samn, you still look tired. You tossed and turned in the bed all night.'

'Yeah,' said Samn. 'I had quite a dream, if you

could call it that,'

Samn rolled over in the bed again after breakfast.

'We have to go to Westminster today, to Parliament square. I am dreading it a touch. I won't find out what we need to do until we get there. I prefer to be less public. At least when we are up on the heath we are not observed. But there's no way of getting out of this.'

'If we look like loonies we look like loonies,' resolved Isobel. 'As long as we evade capture, I don't much care what anyone thinks. Besides, look at the other night. No one cared what we were up to. London is like that. You could be demonstrating naked wearing a snorkel and flippers with a flowerpot on your head and they wouldn't care. They only care when you make them late for work.

'So, Samn. Do you have any idea of what we have to do today?' asked Isobel.

Samn picked up the knife and showed it to her.

'I am not sure if I want to touch it again,' said Isobel. 'I mean, I am happy to assist you, but there's something weird about that knife that makes me feel somewhat nauseas.'

Samn held the knife up and showed the spine of the blade to Isobel.

The gold script contorted into a sentence. 'Hello Isobel,' It read.

Isobel made a face as though she was very taken aback by the blade.

'Well, that's different. It's kind of cool,' she said.

Samn flipped the knife over.

'Thank you for helping our friend,' it read on the other side.

'No problem,' said Isobel in an open reply to the knife. 'There's nothing wrong with a little shifting and changing. I suppose I had better get washed and dressed so we can get going.'

'Good plan,' said Samn.

'Are we bringing Brian?'

Samn looked over at Brian. He covered his head with his paw.

'He looks like he doesn't want to go, but I expect he has to. I will leave it up to him. He's probably got to come and watch.' Samn made a showy, pantomime style point with his index finger, rubbing it on Brian's nose.

'And if you're coming into the centre of town,' said Samn, 'You're going to have to go on a dog lead so as not to seem too conspicuous.'

Brian huffed.

Samn got up and headed for the bathroom. He jumped into the shower beside Isobel.

'Let's have another shower later, a better one,' said Samn flirtatiously.

'Okay,' relented Isobel. 'I see no opposition to that idea. Do you know what you need to bring with you today?'

'To be on the safe side, I will bring more kit from the voodoo shop along with that wacky dagger. Honestly, I can hardly get a minute's peace to molest you properly! There's no rest for the wicked, I suppose.'

'I'll second that!' exclaimed Isobel. 'I nearly had a go on you last night in your sleep, but had a momentary attack of conscience. Hopefully that kind of moral conscience will eventually fade away with regards to you. I would like to be able to take advantage of you, no matter what state you are in.'

Now dressed, the two headed out of the flat. They walked along the tree-lined street, towing Brian along on a lead. Brian didn't act seem enamoured with the prospect, so they did their best not to hurry him too much.

The three stopped at a nearby bus stop and read the bus timetable as they waited for any double decker that was bound for Central London.

'There's no point in taking the car in to central London,' said Isobel. 'You can never get parked.'

As the bus arrived, they boarded the entrance at the back and skipped up the stairs to the second level.

Isobel and Samn sat side-by-side on one of the bus benches whilst Brian settled on the floor underneath them. Isobel bent down and scratched Brian's head.

'You can't watch much down there Brian,' taunted Isobel.

Brian sprang up and hopped up on to the empty seat behind them. Defiantly he began staring out the window and sniffing at the slice of a window that was wedged open at the top.

'Are you watching the watchers now, Miss Izzy?' teased Samn.

Isobel didn't answer, she was distracted by the newspaper headline of a free newspaper sitting on the empty bus seat in front of her. Emblazoned in capitals across the top it read:

"BLOODBATH: GEOLOGISTS SLAUGHTERED ON HAMPSTEAD HEATH!"

Isobel clenched the paper tightly with both hands and read it intently. Her expression filled with an increasing horror. She read on:

'Two senior members of London's Geological Society were torn limb from limb at approximately 8 p.m. last night on Upper Heath, Hampstead, North London. Gustave Roberts, 45 and William Watts, 53 were both attacked by a group of unidentified assailants near Jack Straw's Castle car park. It is believed they were headed towards Heath House to give a scheduled lecture. Rory Levene, 33 escaped the attackers but is still in critical condition in Royal Free Hospital, Hampstead. He is helping police with their enquiries. In a statement from Mr. Levene, he was quoted as saying:

"Everything happened so quickly. One minute we were walking towards the lecture and the next thing I knew something was on top of me, trying to bite my face off. Gus and William were ripped apart by our attacker in a matter of seconds. That's when my panic mode must have set in. I barely remember running towards Heath House. I had so much blood in my eyes I still can't believe I found the door."

The newspaper read ~turn to page 7.

Hurriedly, Isobel began to flip forward to the seventh page.

Samn put his hand down over the paper to steady Isobel.

'You don't need to read that, Isobel,' Samn said softly.

'What do you mean? Why don't I need to read that?' There was a faint rising sound of dread in her voice.

'I am not going to mince words with you Isobel. I am not going to insult your intelligence,' said Samn bluntly. 'But, we did that.'

Isobel began to babble as she spoke.

'But, but we were in all night! What, what do you mean we did that?'

Samn put his arms around her and shushed her with a comforting force.

'We made werewolves,' he said quietly.

'What?!' Isobel bellowed her reply with a blast. It made everyone at the front of the bus jump. They turned around to briefly stare, then went back to ignoring her.

'What the fucking fuck do you mean we made werewolves?'

Samn shushed her again. He carefully tried to push her lips together comically 'Shhh, lower your voice. Look, we did a good thing. I promised it would be a good thing and it is. Don't be alarmed.'

Isobel started to look overwrought by this new turn of developments.

'How the fuck are werewolves a good thing? There's two dead geologists and one in critical condition in the hospital!'

Samn gave her a half-serious look. He then made an over-inflated frown.

'London needed new werewolves.'

'Why the shit-cupboard would London need werewolves? What the fuck-cabinet are you talking about?' garbled Isobel.

'Isobel, Isobel, you need to calm down. Your swearing is getting all out of whack,' replied Samn.

Isobel shook her head. She huffed and stared out the bus window for a moment. She looked at the street below and watched random Londoners as they walked along the pavement, ambled in and out of shop entrances and got on with their lives. She turned around to look at Brian, who sat behind her sniffing out of the window.

'Did you know about this? Do you approve of this?' she addressed Brian. The sound of frustration governed her voice.

Brian looked at her and let out half a bark. A woman in an Indian sari on the opposite seat of the bus looked at Isobel oddly. Isobel registered that woman was witnessing Isobel as she held a conversation she with a dog.

Isobel scanned the woman and their eyes shot towards each other, but neither spoke. She then turned back to Samn.

'Oh, great. We are already on the path to the public thinking that we are mental. Well, that's handy,' sighed Isobel.

'Listen, if I say it's a good thing, it's a good thing. And I mean it,' Samn whispered solemnly to her. 'I had been campaigning with my bosses for quite some time to implement this kind of course of action. My first proposal was to release 6 prides of lions, 20 packs of wolves, 30 hippos and 96 tigers throughout London to aid the weeding out any of the extraneous negative populace and, also to help cull back some the Darwin aspects residing in city as a side project. But, they axed that idea. They said wild animals would be too easy to catch and that the Darwin aspect ratio of the populace was too high to be fair.'

'So, they approved werewolves instead?' enquired Isobel incredulously.

'No, no, no-no-no,' said Samn. He waved his hands in the air, signalling 'no'. 'This new advancement has nothing to do with that old campaign. With that said, I still think this approach is going to work out quite well. This looks as though it will my serve my directors' purposes quite efficiently.'

'What purposes?' she said.

'The werewolves have been deployed for combat,' he replied.

'That is ridiculous!' she whispered back to him. 'Combat? They have eviscerated three nerdy geologists,' lamented Isobel. 'That hardly sounds like a fair fight. What are you trying to say? Are you claiming that they were evil geologists?'

'Would it help for now?' wavered Sam.

'Is it true?' she glared.

Samn looked at her sideways and scratched his ear.

'Not really but, yeah sort of. I mean if you want to get into the semantics of cause and effect then yeah. They were ultimately evil. Their deaths were certainly not in vain by any standards of the imagination,' Samn continued after a short pause. 'They were very valid, in fact. In terms of how I dealt with the situation, well, the directors left it up to me. So, I decided to choose this as a solution and I think it's going to be very effective. You know, it's a bit complicated to try to explain, but my bosses don't like to get involved with the details about how a plan is deployed and executed. They believe in free choice. So, if I project a viable solution, they are usually happy with whatever I devise.'

Isobel looked at him for a very long minute. He could see that she was turning over the possibilities in her mind. Soon, a look of resolve formed in her mind. She exhaled loudly.

'Who are these directors, exactly?' she asked him.

'Very important people, big wheels,' he answered. 'If they need something done, there's a good reason for it.' Samn stared into her eyes as though to entreat her to believe him. She looked back at him and felt a little bit of compassion. She decided she would accept what he had said.

'I still feel a bit bad though,' she mumbled.

Samn piped up with a more cheerful sound in his voice.

'You know those two pervy voyeuristic guys from the picnic blanket yesterday?' started Samn. 'That was them! They were the ones in the car park in the news! Now they can spend a lot more time up on the heath - in nature, enjoying life as werewolves. They can be out in the fresh air a lot more as well. That's nice, isn't it? Nor will they be able to tell anyone what they saw us get up to yesterday. That's good too, isn't it?' There was an irreverent tone of irony in Samn's voice. 'They did seem to like being outdoors. So... I don't really see the overall harm. Not in the long term, anyway.'

Isobel folded her arms.

'Still not happy,' she huffed.

Samn tried to put his hand out to hold hers, but she pulled it away.

'You know what Giacomo Casanova once said to me?' started Samn.

'No, what did he say?' replied Isobel, still miffed. 'In fact, don't bother telling me. I don't care what he said,' she replied with irritation.

'Listen, please don't be angry. Right now, it may seem like we did something bad, but we didn't really. I promise, when you see the bigger picture it will be for the best. Look, this is our stop.' Samn got up and took Brian's lead. Brian jumped off the bus seat. He followed Samn who in turn grabbed Isobel's hand and carefully guided them all down the tiny spiral staircase to exit the bus. A huge imposing view of the Houses of Parliament flanked by Big Ben's clock tower loomed into view beside the banks of the Thames River.

Thousands of tourists bustled around the landmark. They meandered around the square in random groups. Many of the throngs of people seemed to stop every few feet to photograph every object in sight. Samn surveyed the scene of tourism chaos. It comprised of a horde of zig-zagging stray foreign nationals. That were clucked around Parliament square excitedly. The scene was accented by an occasional daub of a white-haired, conservatively dressed Parliamentary-shaped bods. Armed police officers stood beside every gate.

'If you added a few more elephants and clowns, this would make a fine circus,' Samn jibed, trying to lighten Isobel's mood.

Isobel stifled a little laugh. Her eyelashes fluttered as she returned a smile.

He kissed her on the cheek.

Samn, Isobel and Brian crossed the street. They walked towards the park in the centre of Parliament Square and began to head to a less busy part of the field.

The two chose a seat furthest away from the slew of tourists who swarmed the opposite end. Samn tied Brian's lead to a bench. Brian sat up expectantly and started to look around. Isobel and Samn sat down. Samn rifled through one of the bags he had been carrying to try and find the knife. He took it out of the bag and settled it on his lap. He looked down at the spine.

'Good show, yesterday! Mission accomplished!' wrote the knife.

'Yeah,' returned Samn. 'Let's not talk about that right now. Isobel is still pretty cross with me about that.'

The knife printed out another message in script. Samn showed it to Isobel.

'Well done Isobel. Thank you for your help!' The words were printed across the opposite side of the knife's spine.

Isobel looked at Samn. She was still somewhat flummoxed about the way the blade could communicate with them. Samn motioned for her to answer the knife, regardless.

'So, what are we doing today?' she said.

'Building another portal,' printed out the knife.

'Today you are going to make vampires.' The knife twisted itself to turn over in Samn's hand. 'What better location for a vampire portal other than Parliament?'

'If the vampires despatch some of the useless members of Parliament then, I approve,' replied Isobel.

Samn studied the knife with a raised eyebrow.

'I think, Isobel, am I correct in guessing that...?' started Samn.

'Yes' printed out the knife on its' spine. 'The parliamentarians will *be* the vampires. We are modifying the old duffers in the House of Lords in a similar vein.'

'Vein, ha, I doubt they will notice any difference,' Isobel commented.

'Oh, they will notice it,' countered Samn. 'The situation of being a vampire is awful. They live constantly obsessed with their next fix. They are on the run from every corner of sunlight. They are nothing like classical literature. They are not those pale, romantic creatures of the dark. Vampires are afflicted by experiencing something like a death that they can never die from. Plus, due to their constant hunger they have no friends, they literally suck the life out of everyone. They are like reality tv stars. They always smell a bit mouldy too. They are repellent to everyone around them and to each other. I assure you, it won't be pleasant for them, even if it is somewhat deserved. I also agree with you Isobel. I don't half wonder myself if they will really notice. It might take them a while to work it all out, though.'

Isobel rubbed her hands together agreeably. 'Actually, I am quite up for today's task.'

'Good,' wrote out the knife. 'Samn knows what to do. Just follow his lead.'

'Yes, I have a reasonable idea about how to start. We have to draw out another square on this grass,' added Samn. 'The first time that we walk round the square we have to sprinkle the holy water all the way around the far edges. Stick to the grassy bits. You start left and I will go right.'

'Okay, then what?' asked Isobel.

'Well, let's just do this first and meet back here,' replied Samn.

Samn produced two bottles of water from his bag and deposited the knife in the bag in place of them. The couple commenced, slowly pacing around the square in opposite directions, sprinkling holy water on the ground as they walked. Isobel had untied Brian from the bench. She towed him along behind her on his dog lead. He sniffed at the ground as the holy water splashed onto the grass.

With the square finished, they both returned to the original bench and sat down. Samn produced the knife again from the bag. Across the spine of the blade it read.:

'Now all you have to do is follow the holy water path again with the blade pointing down towards the earth. When you are done, stab the ground as close to the centre of the square as you can possibly manage. It's not an exact science. Close enough will do.'

It flipped over one last time.

'Then, you will be all set,' printed the knife.

Samn took Brian's dog leash. He handed the dagger to Isobel.

'Why don't you do it, Isobel? You have the stronger will to fuel this ritual than I do, and its good practice for you as well.'

'Why yes, for this instance I do indeed if I follow what you mean. I hate those cheating bastards in there anyway. If this is one chance to give them a taste of their own medicine in their sheltered asshole lives, then I accept.' Isobel put her hand out. 'The knife, please,' stated Isobel. Samn laughed as he handed her the dagger. He had identified a demented type of glee in her voice.

Samn resolved to leave it until a different time to consider asking Isobel further about her issues with the British Government. He could hear an underlying fury in her voice when she spoke about the subject. He made a mental note to himself to ask her about that sometime.

Isobel glanced at Samn and motioned for him to notice the sporadic sets of police who stood guard at random positions around Parliament.

'What if the police see the knife and try to disarm me?' addressed Isobel.

'Just tuck it up your sleeve,' answered Samn. 'The knife is still pointing towards the earth. It doesn't matter if it can be seen or not.'

'Oh,' said Isobel, tucking the knife up her sleeve. She then proceeded to walk.

Isobel commenced around the square. She held the knife downwards as she paced around the park.

She returned to their bench. Samn stroked Isobel's hair as she sat down.

'Are you feeling a bit better about all of this?' he asked her.

'Yeah,' she replied. 'I had a little time to think. I decided that none of the consequences matter.'

'Okay, well. Let's do this last bit, then we can go.'

Isobel and Samn ambled to the centre of the park. Brian trailed behind on his dog lead. The park still felt very exposed and open to Isobel, but she pushed herself on. The bright blue sky and blazing sunshine made Isobel feel even more conspicuous. The couple walked to the centre of the park and agreed on a central spot in the ground. Samn looked towards Isobel, giving her a nod. She raised the dagger high above her head in the glittering sunlight and violently stabbed the earth. She pushed the dagger with great force into the earth. Part of the hilt had wedged itself into the ground.

A disembodied female voice rang out from the knife.

'And, that's the last of the sunlight those pricks will ever see,' said the voice enigmatically. The voice then chuckled.

Samn, Brian and Isobel watched as the knife plummeted into the earth and disappeared.

Samn noticed someone approaching out of the corner of his eye. An on-duty metropolitan police officer beset the trio.

'May I ask what you two are doing?' enquired the officer.

'Oh, we are just practicing for a play,' said Isobel with a deadpan smile. 'Macbeth.'

'Well, I suggest you go do that somewhere else,' answered the policeman with an authoritative and dismissive glare.

Isobel put Brian's lead into Samn's hand.

'Yes, sir,' she replied. 'We will just be getting off now, thanks.'

Isobel pointed out a bus stop that was nearby and pointed towards it.

'Hey look, there's our bus!' she hollered. Isobel ran ahead to hold the bus up for Samn and Brian. They quickly caught her up and tumbled into the vehicle. Breathlessly, the three stomped up the stairs as the bus trundled along the roads that would take them back to Hampstead Heath.

Chapter 8 Bubble's Pizza

Soon arriving home, Samn flopped down on the couch exhaustedly. Brian skulked into the bathroom and began drinking from the toilet bowl. Isobel scurried to shoo him away.

'No, Brian!' she scolded.

She quickly filled a large bowl of water for him from the tap in the kitchen and put it down on the floor. Brian proceeded to lap up the water. Isobel returned to the bathroom and turned on the light. To her surprise, her two kittens were lolling around in the bathtub. She thought that either she had forgotten to turn off the tap, or that they had managed to turn it on themselves. She noted how cute it was that they were having so much fun waving their tiny front paws under the dripping tap. She felt a fleeting wish that she could be entertained by simple things like that. Perhaps then, a lot of her choices in life may not have had to have been so complicated.

Isobel lifted the two tiny balls of fluff and set them down by the bowls in the kitchen. Upon further inspection, she decided that all the bowls could do with a thorough clean and fresh food. The cats looked up at her with dismay as she removed the bowls. Samn melted into the sofa as he listened to Isobel buzzing around in the kitchen. She tidied the bowls and put the kittens' food on the floor.

Isobel returned to the living room. She handed Samn one of a pair of large glasses filled with gin, orange juice and ice. She also flopped down on the sofa beside him and arranged herself. She sat crossed-legged. She took a big gulp of the gin.

'So, how long will it be before we start reading about vampire crimes in the papers?' The question Isobel had posed to Samn was full of vacant tonality.

'Well, it could be tonight, or it may take a day or two to catch on. It's never an exact science,' he replied. He clinked his glass to Isobel's.

'I wonder what will happen tomorrow.' Isobel's eyes widened with a faraway stare. Then, visibly putting that thought behind her, she announced. 'Oh well, let's order a pizza!'
That was something about Isobel that Samn had swiftly grown to adore. She never seemed to hang on to her emotions for all that long, no matter what they were. He noticed that she always seemed to be live in the moment. She had a quick way of aiming forward towards the new moments.

Brian walked through from the kitchen and lifted his snout towards Samn's ear. He snuffled at Samn's ear loudly, then cut off his snuffle with a sharp exhale.

'Brian has informed me that he wants us to order him his own personal pizza,' said Samn.

'I think we can stretch to that,' chuckled Isobel. 'But this won't be all the time. Dogs need healthy food. This is just a treat.'

'He says he wants a bacon cheeseburger pizza.'

'Well let's get two of those then,' she resolved.

Isobel lifted the handset of her house phone and began to dial. Isobel had used the same pizza delivery service for years. A foreign voice came on the line and spoke in a single sentence with no inflection.

'Hello, bubbles pizza may I take your order please.'

'Oh!' reacted Isobel, 'This isn't Pizza Island? Have you changed hands?'

'This is Bubbles pizza may I take your order please?' replied the monosyllabic voice at the end of the line.

'What's going on?' said Samn.

'I phoned my regular number but they are not my normal pizza people. I know I dialled the right number. They say they are Bubbles Pizza now. I think they may have sold the business to someone else.

What do you think we should do?'

Samn took the receiver from Isobel's hand.

'We'll have two large bacon cheeseburger pizzas, please.'

'Would you like the party special? You get chips, garlic pizza bread, a bottle of soft drink with party special for same price.'

'Yes, okay then, whatever,' replied Samn.

'50 minutes,' said the voice before hanging up.

Isobel looked at Samn with slight confusion.

'He didn't take our address. But perhaps they have it saved linked to my phone. Maybe they still have the old database from Pizza Island.'

'I'll try and ring them again.' said Isobel as she redialled.

Isobel listened as the phone rang on the other end. The same monosyllabic voice came on the line.

'We have your address, Isobel,' said the monosyllabic voice. The phoned clicked and the line went dead.

Isobel looked at the receiver of the phone before

placing it back in the cradle.

'I guess they must have the old database like you said. I hope their pizzas aren't shite,' she added.

'I am sure it will be fine,' countered Samn. 'It's just pizza. If these new pizza people are shite, I have no doubt Brian will eat them both and we can order something else. It's been a long day sexy lady, so let's not worry too much about the details.'

Isobel lifted the remote control from the couch. She turned the television on to a main news station.

'I want to see if there is anything else in the news about the werewolves,' she announced. 'I like to keep abreast of world events.'

The television showed a news reporter standing on the heath by Hampstead ponds.

Underneath him scrolled the headline, 'Second brutal slaying in Hampstead, North London.'

Isobel shot Samn a look of ironic contempt before turning up the sound to listen to the report. A man wearing a fitted, dark blue overcoat and red tartan scarf spoke in a serious, matter-of-fact tone. There was a hint of straining in the way he spoke.

'At around 8 o'clock last night, three people were mercilessly attacked - killing two and leaving one in critical condition in a North London Hospital. Thirty-three year old Rory Levene survived the attack but has been unable to identify his assailants. Tonight, four further victims have been brutally slain near Hampstead Heath's historic men's bathing pond. Police are asking the public to contact them with any information which may help to identify both the victims or the perpetrators of this senseless killing. The motive for these attacks is not yet known. What we do know is that these are vicious attacks. Residents have been advised to stay away from the heath until further notice. At approximately six pm this evening, four men were found brutally dismembered in the changing rooms at Hampstead men's bathing pond. A trusted source revealed to us that several parts of the victims' bodies had been scattered around the vicinity of the changing block. Many large bite marks on the victim's bodies were witnessed by an unnamed local resident who discovered the initial carnage. He was quoted as describing the scene to 'something you would normally see on a battlefield.' There is further speculation that wild animals may have either escaped, or have been accidentally released from a private zoo. London Zoo are assisting with identification if an animal is confirmed to be carrying out these attacks. However, the police are stating that they are not ready to rule out the possibility of a terrorist act … or of this tragedy … being possibly the work … of a serial killer.

Again, the police are asking for any information you may have to be referred to their hotline immediately and for those residing in and around the North London area, to please lock your doors and windows and avoid the heath after dark. The victims' names will be released when they have been identified and we have established contact with their next of kin.'

Isobel stared at Samn sardonically.

A phone number and email address was written across a prompt that ran along a red strip on the TV screen below the reporter. Isobel lifted the phone. 'I'm going to call!' she said ghoulishly. Samn grabbed the telephone receiver from her and slammed it back on the cradle.

'No, you are not!' he boomed.

'But I do have information!' she exclaimed with a cheeky grin. 'I was only going to mention it to them, that we went up the heath yesterday, had a sex picnic and turned everyone watching us into a bunch of werewolves.'

'That's what they call wasting police time, luvvie,' countered Samn.

'It's only wasting their time, if it's not true,' said Isobel studiously.

'Well good luck then, getting them to swallow that bundle of facts. Brian and myself will be here eating pizza when you get back from making your statement at the police station. That is, if they don't decide to section you first.'

Isobel knocked back the rest of her gin and orange.

'You know I am not going to call them, I was just teasing. I am not going to grass you or Brian up. You say you did it for a good reason. From what I saw today, I am prepared to give you the benefit of the doubt,' Isobel spoke in a slightly crazed way as she continued.

'I mean, maybe they were evil geologists like you said. Maybe those bathers at the ponds were evil too!' she added sarcastically. 'They could well have been drug smugglers supplying the local kindergartens and language schools. Or perhaps they were all trafficking immigrant pygmy gay hookers. Who knows? Obviously, they were doing that, that would be the only thing that could justify a sunny afternoon's gambolling across the heath, followed by partial cannibalism with a dismemberment chaser.'

Samn started to laugh. 'You know, you seem to be adjusting to this new mind-set with the greatest of ease, and the mildest of sarcasm to match.' He kissed her on the top of her head.

'Samn, Can I ask you a question, seeing as you are now driving around in my ex-boyfriend's body?'

'Yes, you can. Oh, I see, he's your "ex" now.

Since when did he become your "ex"?'

'The other day,' she said disconnectedly. 'Just after the fireworks when we had sex. Want I want to ask is that if you are inside of his body driving his corporal being around, as such … do you think you have retained any of his memories, or emotions?'

'Possibly,' replied Samn.

'So, if you have got any of his memories or emotions stored in your memory. Can you tell me this? Did he love me, at all?'

Samn stared up into the left-hand corner of the ceiling. She could see he was searching through his mind. 'Yes, yes, I think so,' he said. 'But you can't look at it as generally as that. He loved you like he loved chocolate or roller coasters. It was never in him to feel things any more deeply beyond that. That's as far as his brand of love could ever stretch for anyone or anything.'

'You make him sound like a bit like a bimbo,' replied Isobel with a sad lilt in her voice.

'Well. I want to say is "If the shoe fits …" But truthfully, there's no point in poking holes in someone with diminished emotional capacity. That's the real reason why you two weren't getting along. I had been observing the situation for some time. I was patiently waiting for the right opportunity to find my way in.

And I could see by the way you loved him that the affection was weighted in his favour. The way I have observed you, I could see that you were of a type of mindset that would protect a lover if they had committed a major crime or murdered someone. You always seemed like the type of person that would jump off a ship to save them if they were drowning, even if it meant you might drown yourself. I got the measure of you a long time ago. I could also see it being wasted. Which also made you a perfect candidate for my project.' Samn cleared his throat. 'But with your former companion, those concepts were not available to his emotional consciousness. Those neural pathways in his mind never formed. So, there's no point in being upset with him about it. With more information about his thoughts at the time, I am sure you would have been better able to make better decisions.'

'Yes, we had differences of opinion about the different things we believed in, as well. That could cause us a lot of friction sometimes.' Isobel sounded maudlin. 'He felt there was nothing out there in the universe and I always believed that there was ... something, out there. To me it was indescribable and not documentable, but existent. I had always hoped our differences of opinion would eventually balance us both out to an even keel in some way, but it never did.'

'And you were correct. You shouldn't feel sad. I can reiterate that you did the best you could. His polarity of view wasn't wrong and neither was yours. After all, how boring would the world be if we all believed in the same things? Look at it this way. Look at the kittens, they are a very good example. If you like kittens, you will actively go out and bring them into your life. You'll feed them and put your energy into them and ultimately because you love them they will bring you a lot of joy and an added dimension that only animal admirers will understand. But if a person doesn't like kittens, they will do everything they can to keep them away from themselves, as kittens are nothing to do with how they want to experience their life on the earth. Kittens aggravate people who don't like them. It's better for them to go through life with their own choices and to not have to own kittens just because everyone else says kittens are great. It's also better for the kittens to not have to share oxygen with such miserable assholes. Their act of choosing not to have pets brings them a type of equilibrium also. The important thing to remember is that you have a choice. And it is respected by the universe that if you want nothing to exist in your reality of that nature, then that is how it shall be. If you want something beyond yourself to exist, that shall also be respected and acknowledged. You get to go to the future you devise for yourself.'

Isobel picked up one of her kittens and kissed the top of its' furry head.

'People who don't like cats *are* assholes.'

Samn sighed.

'It's not their time to like the kittens. Maybe next time it will be their time … or maybe never. Overall, it really doesn't matter, because they are not you and you have your own future to be progressing with. So, the best point of view you can have about your former paramour is this. If he was an actor auditioning for a leading role in a film about your life, he was simply miscast.'

'And what about you?' said Isobel, frowning.

'I think you're a hot bitch,' replied Samn. Isobel put her kitten down, and she scuttled away. She turned her body towards Samn and stuck her tongue in his ear. She then playfully pinned Samn to the sofa, pulled up his shirt and began to lick his belly. Samn giggled.

'That tickles!' he exclaimed.

Isobel dragged her nails along the length of his torso, leaving a long set of bright red, raised scratches on his skin. She unzipped his trousers and impaled her mouth forcefully on his stiffening cock. Samn lay back, writhing at the sensation of Isobel's impossibly warm, slippery mouth as she gently ran her teeth along the shaft of his penis.

'You must be hungry,' quipped Samn.

'Yeah, where is that pizza?' replied Isobel.

Brian (who had been lying in the hallway) pricked up his ears and began to bark at the front door. The shrill sound of the door entry phone resounded throughout the flat.

Isobel jumped up. She darted towards the entry system telephone in the hall.

'Talk about timing! That must be pizza!' she said to Samn.

Samn looked down to survey the unfinished state of aching from his erect cock. He pulled his trousers up around his waist.

'We'll come back to that other matter later,' announced Isobel from the hall.

Isobel buzzed in the pizza delivery man. By the front door, she could hear something that sounded like a crash come from the street below. Curiously, she walked out into the communal hallway before turning to look back behind herself. She shooed her two nosey kittens away, motioning for them to go back inside the flat. They retreated into the bedroom and tentatively watched her from a distance. She looked down at the street below.

'Samn, you need to come out here and see this,' she said excitedly. 'There's about ten pizza bikes outside, plus a pink limousine. They are doing bike stunts just in front of the flats. I have never seen that before!' Samn walked out of the flat to join her in the communal hallway to witness the odd spectacle.

'Perhaps nine other people in your block ordered pizza at the same time,' countered Samn.

'What about the limousine?' replied Isobel with a childish tone of excitement.

'Maybe someone is having a party,' replied Samn.

'Oh,' said Isobel. She responded to the buzz of the second entry door system, by walking back into the hallway to let the pizza delivery man in. Samn and Isobel waited at the front door expectantly.

An enormously tall, vivacious-looking older drag queen in a pink spangled dress sporting a huge bouffant blonde wig turned the corner and strode towards them. Isobel and Samn looked at her with their faces full of surprise.

The drag queen sashayed towards them theatrically, with her arms out to greet them. A crew of young men followed behind her.

'Okay, boys,' announced the drag queen. 'They're in. Let's get this kit moved in pronto!' She clapped her hands together directing the young men towards Isobel and Samn.

Isobel and Sam stood aghast as the drag queen, followed by a procession of pizza delivery boys filed past them in the hallway and stood crowded together in their living room. Sam and Isobel followed and stared at them in shock.

'Are you Samn?' said the drag queen.

'Err, yes?' he replied with an air of uncertainty.

'Well, I am Miss Bubbles LaWhore, but you can just call me "Bubbles" or "Bub". And I am here to deliver your pizza, and I am here to sing you a song!'

Bubbles produced a harmonica from the recesses of somewhere in her massive bosom. She blew into the harmonica once, as though to set the pitch. Each pizza delivery boy that stood behind her produced a kazoo from their jacket pocket. All were poised, ready to make a musical accompaniment to Bubbles impending song. Bubbles then sang in the campest style of music hall crooning imaginable. She began.

"Thank you Sam – Merci, Isobel,
we know your job might seem miserable.
But all your deeds aren't invisible
we thank you for your time!

Thank you, Brian, pervy nosey dog,
you've got no part in the dialogue.
We'd like to add you to our catalogue
or epilogue. Thank you for your slog oh dog,

Oh, lovely Brian the dog!

There's still one thing that we need of you …
an honour bestowed upon all too few …
to give two tarts like you a fucking clue
I am relieved you are still in your prime. Pizza gram!"

The young men finished their accompaniment of kazoos. They cheered and clapped. Bubbles bowed to Isobel and Samn graciously.

Samn and Isobel stared at Bubbles as she bowed. It had been a tuneless load of nonsense. Samn politely offered a slow clap and was gently joined by a confused Isobel. This was then followed by a second raucous round of applause from pizza bike boys. They filed into the room bearing not only the pizzas Samn & Isobel had ordered but a variety of boxes, bags and equipment, tins, bottles, pots and pans.

'Just set it up here in the middle of the living room,' said Bubbles as she sidled over to Samn. She licked her finger and ran it across one eyebrow.

'Ooh Samn! Now haven't you chosen a nice little mortality for yourself? You're rocking a little hot body right there, aren't you?'

Bubbles ran her pink glittery nails along one of Sam's cheek and reached out to grab Samn by his ass.

Samn politely dodged her grasp. Bubbles snapped one

of her fingers. A pizza delivery boy appeared by her side with a large pizza box which he opened for her. She lifted one of the pieces of pizza out of the box. She held the slice of pizza up in front of Samn's mouth.

'Would you like a bite?' she said in a theatrical attempt at seduction.

'Well, I did, but... you go ahead,' retreated Samn.

Bubbles voice purred with flirtation.

'But darling, you're going to need all the energy you can get for your next task,' tittered Bubbles. She waved the slice of pizza in front of him.

Sam gulped. He suddenly had horrific visions in his mind of being directed to have sex with this overdressed drag queen. She did have her own brand of allure. When she fluttered her giant eyelashes at Sam he found them mesmerizing. He found himself trying to find a polite way to let her know that drag queens were just not his preference. He stepped back a few paces, making a polite attempt to retreat from Bubbles and her slice of pizza.

Bubbles read his face and scowled at him.

'Oh, it's like that? Well, don't worry, baby! We wouldn't want you doing anything you don't want to do. I have plenty of pizza boys for that later, anyway,' she huffed indignantly.

'I wouldn't wish to do you a disservice, Madame Bubbles. You're a very beautiful woman,' he said, trying to reconcile his potential offence to her. Bubbles capitulated.

Two of the pizza boys began to inflate a large paddling pool in the middle of the living room. Another went into the kitchen, opened a pizza box and placed it on the floor. Brian sprang up and headed towards his pizza enthusiastically.

Bubbles inspected the paddling pool when it was fully inflated, and turned to address the two delivery boys.

'That looks fine, so you can start filling it up,' directed Miss Bubbles.

It appeared that one of the delivery men had set up shop in the kitchen and was busily opening tins. He had also set up four huge pans on each of the rings on the cooker and was slowly heating something up.

Soon, a steady succession of delivery men began darting to and from the kitchen. They returned bearing huge catering sized tins of banana flavoured custard and began dumping it into the paddling pool. Some of the custard sploshed out onto the floor. As the paddling pool became three quarters full, Bubbles double clapped her hand and the delivery boys began to file out of the flat. A pizza boy handed Isobel a copy of her delivery order. "Bubbles Pizza" was written along the top of the docket. She looked at it curiously. It looked like a typical standard computerised pizza delivery receipt, except it had additional itemised tins of custard and the words 'inflatable pool' written on the receipt. Isobel turned to address Bubbles.

'What do you want us to do with this?' queried Isobel, with face full of curiousity.

'Hold your horses, honey. I'll get to you in a minute!' Bubbles went back to ogling Samn. With a stripper's skill, she licked her glossy pink lips before she spoke. She continued to ignore Isobel. She seemed to prefer to place her focus on Samn.

'So Samn,' she announced lasciviously. 'We need you and your little friend to put on a very special show for us tonight. Sadly, this show is not for me. Nor is it the kind of show I would have liked to have seen from you either. But, c'est la vie. We all have our jobs to do.'

'Who is the show for?' interjected Isobel.

Bubbles raised her hand to Isobel's face and answered firmly:

'Let me finish,' she retorted. 'We need you and Isobel to treat these wonderful gifts that we have bestowed upon you as your new playground tonight.

We have supplied you with a selection of noise-makers, football rattles, a megaphone, some fireworks and sparklers plus a pantomime horse costume. Use what of it you like but know this- you better make your show tonight more spectacular than ever. You might not see your audience straight away, but they will be along if you succeed in the elevated level of entertainment expected of you.'

'Tonight, you will be making us some new ghosts!' her manner of speaking was like that of a same show host.

'How do you *'make'* ghosts?' said Isobel.

'Now, you just shut your cake hole honey before someone puts an apple in it, and I will explain it to you,' Bubbles snapped.

Isobel was so shocked by her rudeness that she slapped Bubbles across the face. Isobel then felt a second wave of shock. She realised she had just slapped Miss Bubbles across the face. It was not like her to slap a stranger.

'Oh my, I am so sorry Bubbles. I didn't mean to do that!' she said apologetically.

'It's okay. I suppose I might be suffering from a few little pangs of jealousy towards you right now. I expect I will get over it once I have one of those delivery boys down there planted on my face a bit later.' Bubbles glanced around the room, surveying the random party paraphernalia that now filled the flat.

'Don't worry about the mess. My boys will pop round to clear it all up tomorrow morning.'

'So,' said Samn. 'How *are* we supposed to 'make ghosts exactly? I am still a little bit lost about how this plan is supposed to play out.'

Bubbles took a pair of blue plastic spectacles out of her bra and put them on. She now looked more studious and authoritative whilst wearing her glasses.

'It's pretty easy once you know the formula. Our tests have shown that banana custard is the most accurate and closest synthetic form of ectoplasm. All you need to do with this custard, is make enough of a kinky spectacle to attract and awaken the dormant spirits. They will then be trapped into this gloop here in this inflatable pool. You might not know this, Isobel,' Bubbles added, addressing her with a slightly patronising tone, 'but there is a multitude of ghosts lurking around in the shadows on every square foot of London soil. They are the most voyeuristic, nosey, scopophiliac bunch of peeping toms you could ever hope to imagine. They have been acting like this since the beginning of the humans. Trapping them is particularly easy in certain geographic locations. London is one of them. Stockholm is also particularly good for this too, but we chose London. Some of these ghosts have a habit of watching everyone they can with every chance they can get. And it's almost always when you are in the toilet, shower or hard at it during a shag. You know, back in the 1960's when there were all those nude peep shows around the Orgasm Alley area of Soho, we were overrun with pervy ghosts hanging around the strip joints. Lots of entities on our side got sick. We had contracted something like a virus. It contained flu-like symptoms caused by all the nosey psychic activity going on around town. Then the virus spread out, right out, right across the underworld. Consequently, we had to deploy a kind of "soul reaper" to round all the ghosts up, so that we could banish them again. The "soul reaper" plan did work though. That was *my* idea. And thankfully, most of the standard humans buzzing around Soho were on hallucinogenic drugs in the 1960's. The time frame helped a lot, because people were too high to be was phased by the site of a dark-cloaked man chasing after invisible beings with a butterfly net. For us, that was a lucky escape from detection at the time. I was glad that we rounded up all those nosey ghosts. Things have moved on now and we have a better handle on how to produce the right type of ghost, so you have nothing to worry about.'

'Okay, I basically understand how we are going to attract them, and the rest I think I will just mentally put to one side so we can focus on the task in hand,' said Samn. 'But my question to you Miss Bubbles, is how are you going to distribute the ghosts?'

'Oh,' said Bubbles, 'you just leave that to me, I have picked out some really interesting new locations where I can turn them loose. What you need to know is that we need lots of ghosts... just not as many as Soho in the sixties. That was fucked. I don't want that flu again. I nearly died! Oh, hang on,' she said to herself. 'I am dead.' Bubbles sighed and clapped her hands together.

'On that note, I shall make my exit and let you plan your evening out before your pizza gets cold,' said Bubbles politely.

'Wait,' said Samn, 'How will we know we are doing it right?'

'Hmm, that's a good question...' she replied. 'Oh, I know! I just thought of something. Just film it with your phone! If you see little orbs and dots on the film, you'll know you're attracting the ghosts correctly. You need to generate lots of light on your camera screen. That will help you gauge your success rate. Now, night – night, campers,' said Bubbles. 'Samn...you can walk me to the door.'

Samn complied with her wishes as she minced out of the room.

'Sorry again for slapping you Bubbles,' said Isobel in a conciliatory voice.

'It's okay honey, I've been slapped by the best

of them and it hasn't stopped me yet.'

Bubbles walked out of the door, on to the communal landing and disappeared around the corner. Samn watched the street below as Bubbles got back into her pink limousine. A fleet of pizza delivery bikes swarmed away behind the car as it coasted out of view.

Samn and Isobel walked back into the living room. Brian was snuffling above the pre-opened box. He was wolfing down several slices of pizza at once. Isobel picked up an unopened pizza box and set it on the counter.

Isobel spied her two kittens in a corner of the kitchen under the table. They had somehow managed to get covered in custard. Little patches of custard were dotted around in different splodges on their fur. They looked up at her, their cute faces full of tiny guilt.

'I think if we are going to do this, Samn, it might be beneficial if we shut the kittens and Brian in the bedroom. You know, for their own safety,' said Isobel.

'Yes,' added Samn. 'That sounds a better all-round as a plan.'

Isobel lifted the lid on the four slowly simmering giant metal pans on the hob. Under each lid were several litres of custard bubbling away slowly.

'I had better turn the heat off on those' said

Isobel. She turned the cooker knobs to the "off" position.

Samn and Isobel sat down at their kitchen table and opened the pizza box. They each took a slice and began to eat.

Samn looked at her thoughtfully.

'Well, at least we don't have to go out anywhere else, today.'

'True,' replied Isobel in between bites.

'But what about the noise? What about the neighbours?' said Samn furtively.

'I would worry about that,' replied Isobel in her pragmatic tone. 'As long as we don't use the megaphone they supplied us with past eleven pm it's going to sound just like any other Friday night in Camden Town. People are always shouting, singing and ringing ambulances round here at the weekends. No one is going to think twice about the noise.'

'You know, Isobel,' tendered Samn. 'That leather lingerie we bought the other day would be perfect for later. I would love it if you put that on for me tonight.'

'Avec plaisir,' said Isobel. 'I admit. I am feeling a little bit stern today. I don't know where that slap across Bubble's face came from, from me. I am just grateful she didn't clock me one.'

'Bubbles was a good sport, yes,' replied Samn. 'I am still a bit surprised you did that. What she said was a bit rude. I think she meant it as a joke though. Oh well.'

'She'll be rifling through one of those pizza delivery boys' boxes by now,' laughed Isobel.

Samn dragged his hand across Isobel's and they finished eating their pizza.

~

Isobel had a very fastidious way about her. She never liked a mess. If an object had a use, then it also had to have its own place. If it was just extraneous clutter she would find a way to recycle it. To keep order, she would either give things she didn't need away, clean them up and sell them, or, when there was no other option, just put them in the bin. She took the most pleasure in disposing of objects that would give her a negative memory. To some that may seem lacking in sentimentality. In Isobel's view, people could not be defined by an effigy or an object that might hold a brief memory of them. Isobel stored her memories in her mind, not her belongings. And it was because of this premise that after every mealtime Isobel was often compelled to thoroughly clean her kitchen. The thought of the decorations, party detritus and large paddling pool filled with custard was something that Isobel found briefly challenging to her sense of order. Had it not been for the fact that Bubbles had said that the delivery boys would come back to clear it all up in the morning, she probably would have started tidying immediately.

She stood in the living room and stared at the spectacle. Samn walked up to her and ran his fingers along her waist.

'I know you aren't a huge fan of mess, Izzy. Will you please try and let go of your tidiness? This is only for one night.'

'Of course, I will,' she answered emphatically. 'If it all gets too much I can always take shelter in the kitchen.'

'Or the bathroom…' countered Samn.

'Yes, or the bathroom. In fact, I am going to get the bathroom set up. I am going to have it ready so that after all of this, we can hop straight in the shower. That will keep me calm. I don't want to have to think about that later.

'So… will you go get changed now?' coaxed Samn.

Isobel kissed his neck.

'I am on it right now,'

'And how would you like me?' said Samn.

'Oh, you'll see,' replied Isobel with a lewd lilt in her voice. You just hang out here, and set up whatever else you need to. I'll be out in a few minutes. One thing you can do whilst I get ready is to round up Brian and the kittens. Set them up in the bedroom with a water dish and their clean litter box, just in case we get carried away and need extra time for this.'

'Consider it done,' said Samn.

Isobel went to the bedroom to get dressed. Samn began to unpack the items that 'Bubbles pizza' had left out for them in the lounge. A note was wrapped around a bundle of 13 white candles. The note read "Light these now."

Samn set the candles up on a variety of tea plates and what candle holders he could find around the flat. He set them along the spare spaces of the lounge's long windowsill. He set the pantomime horse costume out and tossed it over one of the chairs. He held it up and took a long look at it.

'That thing is not sexy,' he said under his breath. 'Now if that had been a big furry animal costume with a giant head, then maybe I would have considered that, but a pantomime horse is not going to do it for me. That Bubbles is into some freaky stuff.'

Samn looked under the box and observed a collection of BDSM equipment. He took each piece out one-by-one and examined them as he put them on a chair. Riding crops, wrist restraints, a full leather body bag, chains, shackles and leg spreader bars were the first items to emerge from the box, followed by a large coil of soft black rope, a leather arm binder restraint and a feather tickling stick. He picked up a purple feather boa and a rubber teddy bear and set them on the side table. The most alarming device he saw was something that he recognised as a metal chastity cage.

After placing the black leather spiked restraint paraphernalia on the sofa, he began to unpack another one of the boxes. In it were sparklers, fireworks, a banana, a rubber fist, a catering sized half gallon of cherry flavoured lubricant, a whipped cream maker and a box of cream chargers. He looked at them with a slight feeling of trepidation.

He picked up the megaphone and switched it on. It blared at him emitting loud feedback.

He switched it off again and put it back in the box.

'That's a recipe for a noise abatement society visit. I might put that away for now,' he thought to himself.

Overall, there were enough kinky toys and restraint equipment to allow both himself and Isobel to play in any direction they so wished for the rest of that evening. He was impressed by the lengths Bubbles Pizza had gone to accommodate them, apart from the weird horse costume.

The bedroom doored opened. The click-clacking sound of Isobel's black patent 6 inch heels echoed on the tiling of the living room floor. Samn's mouth dropped at the vision she had turned herself into. She was magnificent.

Chapter 9 Mistress Isobel

Isobel stood facing Samn the middle of the living room. Her long hair was trained into a severe pony tail. Her firm white flesh tensed against an ornate state-of-the-art black leather medical style corset sporting matching black garters and a leather bra. Her outfit was embellished with semi-precious jewels. Her tight, black latex fitted miniskirt had a small slit up one side. Leather 'v' straps peeped out from under her skirt, replacing the concept of wearing knickers. Her face was a shock of white, with red glossy lips and the blackest of cat-like eye make-up. Red blush cascaded down her cheeks and huge black lashes fluttered when she blinked. Her stockings were woven into the sexiest lace pattern he could ever have envisioned. Black skulls were woven into the design. Her leather-gloved hands were decorated with ebony encrusted rings in the shape of skulls and devils with jewelled eyes. In one hand, she held a beautifully plaited black French pigskin leather bull whip. It was coiled. A shiny pair of black patent leather boots were tightly sealed to her legs. Isobel put one leg on a table and finished zipping up the boots. The seven-inch heels had one continuous zip that started at the ankle of the boot and stopped just above the knee. Samn had never seen anything more beautiful.

'It's seems that those pizza delivery boys left a few things behind beyond the custard,' said Isobel with a telling smile.

'I'll put the dog away,' said Samn with his face flushed.

Samn shooed Brian quickly into the bedroom. He sourced the location of the kittens, and settled them onto the bed. He dashed to the kitchen and grabbed their water bowl. He set it down inside the bedroom door, which he then shut. He returned to the waiting Isobel who shot him and icy cold, sexy look. Her shiny leather costume seemed to have an effect of transforming part of her persona into someone who seemed to be very focussed. He suspected it might be time to play.

'For the rest of the evening, you will address me as Mistress Isobel. You are now my plaything and I am the audience that you must appease. The first thing I would like to do, is examine my toy, which is you.'

'Yes, Mistress Isobel,' said Samn with a huge grin.

Isobel produced a blindfold from the settee and placed it around Samn's eyes.

'Stop smiling whore boy, and put your hands up,' said Isobel seriously.

Samn was having the worst trouble trying not to smile.

He decided to comply with her wishes.

It wasn't that Isobel wanted him to have a miserable time. But dressed as she was, with Samn taking on the submissive role, she wanted to be able to focus on him as a sex toy. She had always had a serious fetish for sexual objectification. She liked the idea that he was there, and his job was to please her. In past conversations, she had had in fetish bars and clubs with random strangers long before, she knew she wasn't entirely alone in this aspect of her kinky fantasies. She found out from them that a lot of guys had had so little attention sexually from previous partners in that way. She remembered being told one time that the kind of attention they had had, was always centred on the girl being the primary visual sex object in the situation. That effect had proved to make some those fantasies of objectification flourish wildly. Isobel was keen to find out the truth of that theory. To be taken, done with and forced to be an object of pure physical pleasure and no more, was something not enough men had in their lives. Isobel was aware of that.

The way she saw it, every emotion (whether conflicted against being submissive or amenable to the idea) was just another tool in the toy box to play with. To her, a sizable percentage of the kind of sex she enjoyed tended to lean towards the psychological. Thus, adding visual and sensual pleasures to that equation seemed like a promising idea. She blindfolded Samn.

Sightless, stood up straight with his hands on his head. He wondered what Isobel was planning to do. As soon as his sight was taken away, he could feel other parts of his senses begin to take up the slack. Isobel produced a large pair of sharp dressmakers' scissors from a desk drawer and began to cut his clothes off.

The sound of the scissors cutting through Samn's clothing made him feel slightly anxious on two levels. The first feeling was a sense of anxiety that Isobel might slip with the scissors and accidentally cut him. The second emotional response was much greater. He felt enormously exposed and vulnerable. Not being able to see what was happening and making no attempt to stop her was an extremely challenging state of mind. Submitting to Isobel as his Mistress and current decision-maker about his present sexual fate, didn't make him feel weak. It made him feel quite the opposite. He felt that his giving over control to Isobel meant that he had enough dominance over his own mind to allow it to let go of his brain's subconscious programmed desire for constant control of everything that was going on around him. He started to realise that this must essentially be what every submissive enjoys. The power to be strong enough to let go.

The last stitch of Samn's clothing dropped to the floor. Apart from the blindfold, he was now naked.

'Go and lock the front door' said Isobel.

Samn moved to take off his blindfold. Isobel stopped

him.

'I didn't give you permission to remove that,' she said coolly. 'I also want the exterior gate door locked, so you will have to open the front door first.' Isobel sat down on the couch and waited patiently as she observed Samn, still blindfolded, feeling around the key hook for the house keys. She watched with a little smile as he carefully crept his way through the hall and found the front door. Samn found this first task to be a bit nerve-racking. He knew if he opened the door whilst wearing a blindfold and still naked that there was a possibility someone could walk past the door as he was locking it. Being spotted by one of her neighbours with a blindfold on and a huge erection was a considerably nerve-inducing state of mind. If they did see him, he was aware that he wouldn't know saw him. Despite those anxieties he had about completing this task, he persevered.

Samn opened the interior door and felt around the doorframe until he found one of the bars of the gate's exterior door. The chilled air in the hall washed over his naked form. He pulled the gate inwards and slammed it shut. He quickly fumbled around nervously, trying to find the right key to shut the exterior metal barred gate.

A middle-aged woman walked past the gate, she gave him the once over.

'Nice cock,' she said, before walking on. Samn

could feel his face flush with heat. He shut the interior door and locked it, then felt his way back into the living room. There was nothing he could say. He could hear Isobel laughing in the lounge. He guessed she had heard what had just happened.

Still blindfolded. Samn shuffled back into the living room. Isobel stood up and led him to the sofa.

'Get on all fours on the sofa, and wait for me,' she demanded.

Samn bent on all fours as he was asked. He waited for her on the sofa. He listened as the click-clacking of her high heels walked through to the bedroom. He heard her shut the door. With the greatest of quiet, she sat down on the bed and slowly unzipped her crotch length thigh boots to remove them. One of the kittens woke up to watch what she was doing, but soon resumed sleep. Isobel tiptoed back to the bedroom door. She turned the handle and padded back into the hall without making a sound. With the greatest of stealth, she crept into the living room to approach the blindfolded Samn, whilst doing her best not to breathe. With a feather touch, she picked up a leather riding crop, but then put that down again. She decided that her gloved arm would probably be more effective. With one sharp, sweeping movement she lowered a heavy blow on to his backside with the flat of her hand. Samn was so alarmed by the shock of this one hard slap that he thought he had nearly jumped into the air. Isobel rubbed his ass reassuringly.

'I just couldn't resist the opportunity,' she said, smiling to herself.

Isobel went into the kitchen and opened the pot lid of the warmed custard as it sat simmering on the cooker. She lifted the entire pan and brought it through to the living room. It had gone through her mind to lead Samn onto the floor, but she didn't want to ruin the element of surprise. Isobel could hear Samn's short breathes. It told her everything she needed to know about his state of mind. She knew he was starting to experience a heightened state of awareness in his newly acquired human form. This situation was one where she had the advantage. She knew that. Samn wondered with trepidation, what she would do next.

She stood over his naked back and watched herself in what seemed like slow motion, as she tipped the entire pan of warm custard over Samn's back.

He let out a confused yelp. He was so filled with anxiety, that he didn't realise what it was. The overwhelming scent of custard reached his nostrils, and he realised what she had done to him.

Isobel watched with a delighted gaze as the custard slithered down his back and over his ribs. Isobel removed her gloves and started to massage the custard all over his body. She drew something in the custard and sucked the run-off from her index finger. She enjoyed watching Samn's reaction to the sludge running off his frame. It was particularly interesting how the custard had pooled into the crack of his arse and was now using the tip of his penis as a funnel for the custard to escape onto the sofa.

Keeping his blindfold on was infinitely challenging for Samn. He felt like he wanted to rip the blindfold off, ravage Isobel with kisses and have his way with her there and then, but he knew he couldn't do that. He had not been instructed to do that. Once he was past the shock of the initial feeling of having had a large pan of warmed custard tipped over his back, the next few feelings were a little bit out of turn. At first, it felt comforting, because his body was still a little bit chilled from his visit to the front door. Waiting in one position for Isobel had also made his skin feel cold. The second thought was one which he would not share with her; it was a worry about the damage to the upholstery on the sofa, which he knew was nonsense to bother to think about. The next thing that came into his head was wonder about what Isobel had drawn on his back. He couldn't resist asking her.

'I wrote "custard slut" on your back,' Isobel replied. 'I am going to write "Use me" above the word "custard slut" next. Or I may write "abuse the", I haven't decided which one yet. Next time you address me, be reminded that you need to ask for permission to speak.'

'Yes Mistress,' replied Samn.

'You mean "Yes Mistress Isobel",' she said curtly.

Isobel opted to write 'abuse the' above the words 'custard slut'. She then informed him of her choice. She then set about thoroughly rubbing the custard into his back, over his legs and into his hair. His body was now glazed over in a shade of pale yellow slime. The hypnotic motion of rubbing slippery custard over his body compelled her to use it as a lubricant to stroke his cock. She grabbed a large handful of the custard and started to massage the length of his shaft. The oozing warmth, mixed with the feeling of Isobel's two hands rubbing at his cock and balls made him start to feel disoriented and slightly disconnected. Samn found himself even more wobbly as he felt the distinct sensation of Isobel's warm, custard sodden tongue darting in and out of his asshole. He groaned with bliss. Isobel walked into the hallway and found Brian's new dog collar and lead. She returned to the living room and attached it around Samn's neck. She tugged on it tightly and ordered him off the sofa. Kneeling at the base of her arse, she forced his head between her legs and ordered him.

'Lick.'

By this point, Samn felt so turned on, that he was ready to fulfil anything Isobel asked of him. He was midway between an obsessive feeling his mind that screamed to him about his wanting to cum, mixed with trying to stay in control. He felt he wanted to stay in his heightened state of arousal for as long as possible. He partly wished she would order him to cum immediately, but had a feeling that that was unlikely. He could sense that, the longer amount of time that he left it before he reached a climax, then the further away he would be from his brain switching off from its dirty mode. He also knew that if both stayed in 'dirty mode', it would be the best way to achieve the maximum kinky gratification needed to complete their task.

Despite his directives, despite knowing that she was now his Mistress, and that it would be Isobel's decision how and when he would be allowed to cum, he attempted to negotiate a quick release from his torment.

'Mistress, may I cum?' he said brazenly.

'Absolutely not,' replied Isobel haughtily. 'That is a ridiculous question.'

The answer brought a strange feeling of comfort to Samn. It confirmed that he had no choice in the situation. He liked knowing that.

Isobel produced the metal chastity device from the side table. She grabbed his painfully erect penis and gently teased it into place in the cock cage. She then fastened it with a lock and key.

'You will cum eventually, but I will decide

when you cum. You are not allowed to know when or how. That is privileged information. That information belongs to me.'

'I understand, Mistress' complied Samn.

'Now' she said, yanking his lead. I want you to give me pleasure. You may start by licking the base of my toes and working your way up to my ass. Your primary directive is to ensure that you endeavour to please me. If you focus on that and nothing else, I will be happy.'

Isobel pushed Samn's head down in the direction of her feet and removed his mask. She watched as a slippery, dripping, slime-covered Samn began to kiss and lick at her toes. She smiled. He smelled like custard. She sat down on the floor. She raised one foot up and shoved it in his face. Samn carefully began to suck on each toe individually. He watched as Isobel threw her head back in ecstasy. As he bit and sucked at her toes he ran the length of his tongue along the base of her stockinged foot. Abruptly, he bit into her heel. Isobel writhed with pleasure. Watching her enjoyment made his cock harden to the point of feeling like it might burst. The feeling added to his sense of frustration. He knew that if she had the keys to his chastity device there was nothing he could do to bring about his release. After thoroughly kissing both her feet equally, he carefully worked his way up her legs, kissing and gently biting her legs in random patterns. Isobel rolled over on her stomach.

'Do that to the tops of my thighs,' she demanded. Samn complied. He buried his face into her stocking tops and began nipping at her flesh. He couldn't see Isobel's face but he could hear her moans. Her flesh became scorching hot with excitement. The heat began building against his face. She pushed his head into the small crevice between her thighs.

'Now bite my pussy,' she rasped.

Samn immediately buried his face between her legs. The sensation for Isobel, of having her pussy lips bitten was rapturous. Even though Samn was the one locked in the chastity cage, the knowledge of his restraint was just as torturous in Isobel's mind. Because she knew that until she removed the device, she couldn't order him to fuck her. Taking the time to remove the device meant that crucial minutes would be lost from his current mode of pleasing her. In her heightened state of arousal, she was reluctant. Isobel parted her legs to let the full length of Samn's tongue dig deep inside of her pussy. She moaned again and pushed her ass into the air to give Samn better access.

Isobel soon found her excitement to be too overwhelming. She fervently grabbed the keys and unlocked the chastity cage. She leapt up from her position and forcefully threw Samn into the paddling pool full of custard. Dashing to the kitchen, she retrieved another large pan of heated custard from the kitchen and dumped it over Samn. She felt an almost insane compulsion to try and get his cock as far down the back of her throat as she could possibly manage. She felt as though she wanted to eat him whole as she attempted it.

She gagged heavily on his prick but kept on sucking. The rhythmic, repetitive movements of sliding her mouth up and down his cock became almost hypnotic. She felt like she didn't want it to end, but knew in a corporeal sense that it had to at some point. The key was being able to milk those sensations for as long as she could, so she could gain as intense an orgasm as possible. For Isobel, the art of being in control meant she would have the deciding decision about how that would happen.

Samn was transfixed. He couldn't take his eyes away from the spectacle of watching her lips encircling and swallowing his cock repeatedly. He was aching to be given permission to fuck her. His mind had already raced forward to future images of sliding himself hard into her pussy, but Isobel seemed to be in a trance. Dark images jostled in her mind for space as they careened towards a deep chasm of concentrated control. She felt as though she had stepped away from the scene momentarily and was directing both herself and Samn's pleasure from a different point in the room. It felt like a gateway had opened in the deepest recesses of her mind where every dirty fantasy she had politely kept in check was superseded by a more powerful, subconscious drive to embrace only her most animalistic impulses. It made her feel very free.

The altered state seemed to suspend time to her, and she savoured the knowledge that the next thing she would feel, was his cock pounding hard into her, because she would be ordering him to.

'Fuck me, Samn,' demanded Isobel. 'HARD.'

Samn needed no prompting from her order. He watched as Isobel crawled into the paddling pool of custard. She knelt up on all fours, spreading her black stockinged legs wide enough to allow him to enter her.

He observed the beautiful roundness of her bottom but struggled to take his eyes away from her cunt. Grabbing her by the hind quarters he forced his cock inside of her and was surprised that the full length of it slid in immediately. The mixture of warm custard and pussy juice between her legs was just too delicious for him. He reached forward and grabbed a handful of custard from the pool and began rubbing it into her ass.

'Fuck me in the ass, slave,' demanded Isobel.

Samn was delighted by her order. He grabbed the length of his cock at the base and began to work the head of his penis into her tight asshole.

'Now I want you to tell me what you are doing to me, exactly at the time that you are doing it, slave,' said Isobel. 'And I want graphic descriptions.'

Samn endeavoured to comply, but the order felt unfamiliar to him. At first, he felt a mixture of guilt and embarrassment by it. He decided he would persevere with the mental challenge of overcoming his nerves relating to voicing his filthiest actions in detail.

Isobel wriggled her ass in front of him. She then straightened her back.

'Tell me,' she commanded.

'I am, pushing the head of my cock into your tight ass, Mistress,' said Samn.

'Good, go on,' she said.

'And I am trying to force the rest of my cock as far inside of your ass as it will go,' explained Samn.

'That's good. Go on,' she said, cajoling him. 'Now tell me what you are thinking about.'

'I am thinking about wanting to reach out and grab your tits so I can rub custard into them,' he answered. 'And I am deliberating about whether it will feel better to cum inside of your cunt or your ass.'

'Well, I expect they will both feel good, but neither of those choices are up to you. They are up to me,' replied Isobel softly. 'But, for a moment, we have to stop.'

This new directive was more torment than Samn's mind could bear, but he had to do it. She was the boss. He had agreed for her to be so. He felt slightly tenuous about this command from her as he had already worked half of the length of his cock into her ass. The only direction his prick wanted to go was forward, not backwards.

'Why, Mistress?' said Samn

'Oh, you boys can be so forgetful sometimes in these situations, can't you?' she laughed. 'We need to see if what we are doing is attracting enough of an audience or not,' she replied. 'Let me up to get my phone, so I can video the surroundings with it.' She hopped up. Samn, feeling slightly deflated, watched as she tried not to slip on the floor due to her custard-covered stockings. She washed and dried her hands in the kitchen, grabbed her phone out of her handbag, then began to film different random spaces around the room. She then watched back what she had filmed, before showing the recording to Samn. They both studied at the screen.

'I think the it's too overexposed to work out what's going on,' said Samn. 'Maybe we should turn the all of the lights off and film the room again.'

'No,' countered Isobel. 'Look again,' she replied.

They watched the video footage back on the camera

phone for a second time. Tiny streaks and flashes of white light darted across the screen, whilst odd bubbles of light meandered haphazardly around the room. The light was flowing uncannily in the direction of the custard-filled paddling pool.

'That must be a good thing,' said Isobel. 'I think it's working.'

Samn looked down at the paddling pool. He stuck one of his hands into the custard.

'Mistress Isobel,' he said. 'May I request that you turn out the lights momentarily, seeing as you are less slippery than I am right now?'

Isobel went to the light switch. She turned it off.

The custard rippled with a glow of different shades of green. Bright, bioluminescent bubbles formed on the surface of the custard.

'Ectoplasm,' said Samn.

'Well,' said Isobel. 'Whatever we are doing, must then be correct. Therefore, I now order you to resume.' She walked back to the light switch and flipped it on, then resumed her position expectantly on all fours in the paddling pool. She craned her neck around and stared at Samn with a look of impatience.

'Now go back to your graphic descriptions of

what you were doing to me,' said Isobel playfully.

Teasingly, Sam rubbed his cock along her pussy lips.

'I am currently rubbing my cock along the edges of your pussy. Now, I am tightening my grip at the base of my cock. I am now stopping the impulse from thrusting my entire girth inside of your pussy, because I want to make you wait,' he teased. 'Now, I am forcing the head of my cock into your asshole, and I am thinking about shooting my spunk either up your ass or across your back.'

'I like the sound of both those ideas,' replied Isobel.

Because Isobel was facing forward, she couldn't entirely witness the way he was fucking her in the same way that Samn could. But, she enjoyed the way he was describing it to her. It filled her head with a succession of fast, forbidden and delicious images. What he had said to her, made the most luscious and delectably dirty scenes dance inside of her mind when she closed her eyes. It had the effect of a type of bizarre sensory overload. The way she could feel his thrusts from behind, coupled with his voice recounting in detail the description from his perspective, made her brain feel like it was going to fragment into a dreamlike state of pure joy.

She could feel her mind floating off into an altered state. It was a place where everything was focussed on pleasure. The rest of her sense of being alive just seemed to melt away before her. The outside world, who she and Samn were, and every mundane detail about life drained out of her brain to make way for what she knew would be an extremely involved and intense orgasm. She could feel the blood drain out of her head as it descended into her clitoris.

'I can't take any more Samn,' relented Isobel. 'You have to fuck me now, or I am going to lose my mind.'

Samn obliged. He ripped his penis out of her ass and began furiously pumping her cunt. Juices dripped down her legs as he ripped harder into her pussy. Isobel screamed. All previous images and Samn's graphic descriptions crashed together in her mind at high speed. They flashed in front of her eyes with a hastening misrule. She could feel the intense sensation of a savage orgasm building in the base of her skull. She threw her head back and pushed herself back hard on his cock, whilst trying to force it as deep inside of her as it would go.

Isobel moaned and began to yell. She felt a wave of bliss bolt through her from her pussy up to the back of her brain. Her brain felt as though was at the very top of a roller coaster, about to descend into a plummeting spiral. She clenched her fists and observed herself as she involuntarily grabbed out at anything that might be in front of her that she could hang on to for leverage. The pleasure pooled in repeating attacks. It made her feel like time was advancing at different lengths. Samn made a final, violent thrust into her and Isobel shrieked wildly. A high-pitched yelp escaped as she came, and jets of female cum squirted out of her pussy. Samn felt the area all around his thighs get completely drenched with her pussy juice. His world became centred on Isobel with a type of tunnel vision. He felt an uncontrollable urge to cum in Isobel's ass immediately. He took his prick out of her cunt and carried on thrusting into her, feeling his own orgasm build at the base of his cock. Samn shut his eyes. The intense simultaneous visual and physical gratification was too overwhelming for him to witness. Every fibre in his body seemed intently focussed on the last few strokes that would liberate him from his intense torment. He hammered his cock into her ass furiously, then felt a surge of freedom as he shot his load high up into her ass. His mind swirled and for a moment. It felt like embers were flying chaotically around his brain. Columns of pleasure ravaged through his system in waves, working their way rapidly from the end of his prick and then back up into his brain. The mental pictures of everything that he had just done with her played itself back to him before lifting out of the top of his head before floating away. It felt like they were taking off, far into space. He looked down and watched Isobel she squeezed his cum out of her ass. She then gathered it up in her fingers and ran it along her tongue. The two collapsed back into the pool of custard. Both laid in a state of disconnection for a few minutes, not able to speak. Samn soon felt himself coming back to earth. He hugged Isobel and she kissed his neck. The both looked down at the paddling pool around them. Isobel marvelled at the sight of the green glowing mass in wonder.

'I have never seen so much glowing green custard,' she said.

'I have never seen so much cum,' he replied.

Chapter 10 Parliament

Isobel and Samn both emerged from their shared shower and sat down on the bed.

'That was fun!' exclaimed Isobel. 'but I am also glad we don't have to clear that all up.'

'Yeah, me too, because I wouldn't even know where to begin,' he added.

'What time is it?' said Isobel.

'I am not sure, I kind of lost track of time for a while. I am still thinking about what's in all that glowing green stuff in the next room.'

'Yeah,' said Isobel. 'I gave up on questioning things like that a long time ago. You never get time to question anything much, when you live in London. So, let's just get some sleep.'

'Good plan,' he replied, yawning.

The two lay beside each other side in the dark. They both stared at the ceiling in silence. There was an electricity in the air. They were both too wired up to go to sleep but had both reached a kind of quiet stand-off of wanting to digest their new experience in silence. After a short passage of thought in the darkness, Isobel and Samn both managed to drift asleep.

A few hours later, Isobel sat up in the bed, wide awake. Samn seemed to still be in a deep sleep. A young woman in a tight, black satin full length coat with a fluffy collar was watching her from the end of the bed. She was wearing a little black top hat decorated with a black lace veil that cascaded down her face which concealed her features. The woman stared at Isobel quietly. Isobel could make out a half smile through the lace. Two vicious-looking Komodo dragons were crawling at the woman's feet, occasionally growling and switching their powerful tails. The woman held them by a pair of thick leather collars that were attached to a heavy silver chained lead. The chains were split in two.

'Seeing as you decided to wake me up from my sleep Miss Isobel, I thought I might return the favour to you.' The woman's voice was soft, but direct.

'Who are you?' said Isobel, rubbing her eyes. 'Am I dreaming?'

The woman got up and switched on the light.

'That's up to you to decide. The information I need to relay to you is important whether you are sleeping or awake. So please listen,' she said with a cool tone.

'As to who I am, I used to live here, in this flat. But I came to an unfortunate accident. I'd rather not go into the details, as they are particularly unusual. I now exist somewhere else with my companions. It's not very far from here.'

'Well, you look okay to me. I am not sure by what you mean when you say, "unusual accident". I expect if you wished to elaborate on that you would have done so,' said Isobel, still bleary. 'So, is there something I can help you with?'

The woman shifted her position at the edge of the bed. Isobel glanced over at Samn, who was still in a deep sleep.

'Yes, there is. There are some things I have been asked to relay to you about the former Sam. He asked me to speak with you. You have created a new portal in this flat. Having been a previous occupant, it was easiest for me to be the one to come through.'

'Okay, what is the message then?' replied Isobel calmly. She felt slightly irritated but couldn't entirely fathom to herself why she felt that way.

'Your former Sam is not exactly where you think he is. His message is that he wants to be allowed to come back,' said the woman.

'Well, *where* is he then?' said Isobel.

'He *was,* originally where you think went. He was in that loop of repeating the same days over and over, but he's not stupid. He figured out something was wrong quickly. He's very upset about the situation in fact. Ever since, he's been at the viewing windows watching your antics, but unable to comment or intervene. I daresay, he is very irate about it.'

Isobel paused to think for a moment. She could feel her mind quickly shift into a defensive state.

'Oh, dear,' said Isobel with a slight touch of patronage. 'I am sorry to hear that,' she added. 'That's a bit of a shame. He needs to ask himself a few questions about what he had, and what he was doing with it. I feel I was very patient at the time. But I can't honestly say I want to go back to the way things were before. What would be achieved by doing that?'

'I am just passing on a message,' said the woman enigmatically. 'The message is that he wants his life back, and he promises you that he will change.'

She stared long and hard at the woman, studying her whilst deep in thought.

'Tell him I will think about it, but it's my future too. He was fucking with that and I am still pretty pissed off. He will just have to wait for things to get better, just like I did for so many years. Tell him that in those exact words please. Thank you,' said Isobel with a tone of ire in her voice. She felt annoyed even thinking about the subject. 'Are you also saying he cannot come back of his own volition now? Because, if it's up to me, I am thinking, "too little, too late."'

The woman lifted her hands from her lap and reached out to stroke the head of one of the dragons. It let out a deafening growl. The woman didn't react. She carried on stroking his head.

'It's true. No, he can't come back on his own now. He was reliant on you for every aspect of his existence for so long, that you ultimately took possession of his will. His further inactivity in life then caused his soul to slip along with it. He gave it up without even noticing. He regrets it now. So, the ball is indeed in your court.'

'Just be careful what you are getting yourself into. Look first, leap second,' said the woman.

Isobel scratched her head thoughtfully. She breathed for a moment, then prepared to respond.

'Thank you for your comments. I must say I am a little bit sad that he saw all that Samn and I got up to. But in truth, I am not particularly that upset. I have heard so much nay-saying from the former Sam. I have no interest in getting on his merry - go - round to nowhere ever again. I spent many years of my life listening to his negativity garnished with the whys and wherefores when nothing changed. I have now awakened from the bad dream that he was. My time was a precious commodity to me. He pissed that time up the very same wall that I kept banging my head against to try and fix everything between us. I am not feeling charitable in his direction. Every time I tried to suggest some new solution to our problems there was always a reason from him as to why it wouldn't work. Now, I am finding that my new solution is working out just fine for me. On paper, the *form* of Sam is still on the earth. So, it's not like the police will be coming to look for me. And, things are going a lot better for the second Samn and I, as he may have witnessed. The fact that Sam has been detained at an alternate location seems like a very acceptable compromise to me. He kept me in limbo, now he can experience that for a while himself. Tell Sam, that deeds meant more than words to me. From him, I saw none. And if I were to draw up a list of his deeds in regards of doing right by me, they would be almost non-existent.'

The woman let out a heavy sigh. 'I will tell him what you said, but please think carefully about what is going to happen next. It is being viewed that you are in the middle of a type of unusual chess game. You appear to be making some very dangersome moves. You need to be aware of that.'

Isobel copied the woman.

'Dangersome, hmm. Well. I may not know *precisely* what is happening on your side of existence, but I am having a lot more fun than I was before. That has a high value to me, especially after the grinding years of misery Sam provided. Whatever those *moves* you speak of are, I am sure I will be able to deal with the consequences. He needs to understand that if you keep trying to break a person down, eventually they will have nothing left to lose. If that's "dangersome", then so be it. I still question what benefit his kind could really be to anyone on my side. Presently, I believe he is best serving the planet by not being here.' Isobel could feel a well of anger beginning to form in the pit of her stomach, but had kept her voice very even and calm.

'Then it shall be as you wish, Isobel,' whispered the woman. The woman gradually evaporated way from her position on the end of the bed. One of the two Komodo dragons growled at Isobel. Both then quickly faded away. Isobel fell back to sleep.

At about 7 a.m. the entry buzzer went for the door went. Isobel woke up. She clambered out of the bed and made her way towards the entry phone, still half asleep.

'Bon-jour bitches,' said the distinctive voice of Bubbles at the other end of the intercom. 'It's collection time!'

Isobel pressed the buzzer and voiced, 'Thank fuck for that.'

Samn got up and made his way into the bathroom. He shut the door and voiced a few early morning grumbles. Isobel could hear him clanging around in the bathroom.

'I feel like I have a massive hangover,' he shouted to Isobel, though the door.

The buzzer went for a second time and Isobel pressed the entry system to admit Bubbles and her clean-up crew through the second entry door. She then unlocked and opened her door gate to let them all into the flat.

Madame Bubbles sashayed into the room wearing a shocking pink coverall. The words "biohazard" were printed all over the garment. She was followed by four men in white biohazard suits. One of the men carried a wet-and-dry vacuum cleaner. He immediately went into the living room and began to use the vacuum to hoover up glowing-green custard. Another man found the mop and bucket in the kitchen and began cleaning the floors. The third man started packing all the equipment they had dropped off the night before back into the boxes. He lifted the boxes and began ferrying them back to the pink limousine that was waiting for them in front of the building.

Bubbles put her hands on her hips, overseeing the clean-up. Samn emerged from the bathroom looking a bit less sleepy. Bubbles whacked Samn's rump as he walked past her.

'I heard you had a visitor last night, Isobel,' said Bubbles.

'What visitor?' said Samn.

'You were fast asleep,' said Isobel. 'Well, Miss Bubbles. I have to say it seems that you miss nothing.'

'Damn right. I like to be kept informed in my line of work,' said Bubbles. 'I've got eyes on the back of my head, the back of my ass… I've got eyes everywhere baby.'

'What visitor? What did he say?' said Samn inquisitively.

'*She* said a lot of things,' corrected Isobel. 'She quoted various platitudes. She rambled on about this and that. I took some of it in. But really, what I chose to do is my decision. I don't take advice from people I hardly know. I am sure she was only trying to be helpful, but taking advice from a dead person about how to be alive is much like taking marriage advice from someone who is divorced.'

Bubbles let out a little laugh. 'Well, I guess that told her.'

'Where are the rest of those pizza delivery boys?' Samn asked Bubbles.

'Some of them are still in the limo downstairs

with a hangover, much like yours. They are still sleeping last night off. I got very riled up after I left here, and seeing as I had some spare time coupled with the sheer volume of spare cock, everything quickly descended into an orgy in the limo. I had to pay them all, of course. They are efficient assistants but they are still a troupe of dirty little sluts for hire. They'll do anything for a two-quid tip. There were some extra tart boys that I didn't fancy so much, so I sent them to Westminster. They had to dropped off some supplies for the new vampires you created yesterday.'

'Oh, really?' said Samn, 'So I take it the ritual went okay then?'

'Well,' said Bubbles. 'Mostly, well yes and no. There's rather an excess of vampires in Westminster now. We might need your services to thin them out a bit.'

Isobel stared at Samn and Bubbles in disbelief. Isobel dashed over to the television in the bedroom and switched on the news.

'Excess?! Vampires?! I thought we were just making a few vampires, the same way we only made a few werewolves!' she howled.

Isobel stared at the TV screen aghast. Aerial shots of Parliament Square were shown as a headline flashed in red across the bottom of the screen.

"Westminster Siege: chaos as M.P.'s take to streets in bizarre rampage."

Isobel turned the report up. She could feel a sense something ominous sinking into her stomach. Samn and Bubbles observed the television nonchalantly from a slight distance.

A reporter on the TV was standing on a balcony overlooking Parliament Square. Crowds of people were running and screaming wildly. Shots were being fired. Police vans lined the streets. The wavering voice of the reporter spoke.

"Armed service response teams have been gathering in the centre of Parliament Square since late last night. At around 10:30 pm what was thought to be a fight broke out in the sports and social bar at The Houses of Parliament, when MP for Falkirk Raymond Brace attacked 51-year-old Tory Councillor Ewan McDonald. Labour whip Frank Pollard was present and escaped the ensuing battle. We have Mr. Pollard, on the line."

The screen showed a bespectacled, suited man with ginger hair. He was sitting behind a desk. Live pictures of the Parliamentary affray were being shown on a screen behind him.

'Mr Pollard, can you tell us what happened in the Parliamentary bar last night?'
Mr Pollard stared at the camera for a few seconds

before snapping out of his daze. He WAS wide-eyed and in shock. After a few seconds, he began to speak.

"I... I will try,' said Mr. Pollard feebly. I had just finished off some paperwork. I had stopped to meet a colleague for a drink. At, at first, it just seemed like a disagreement that got out of hand between two M.P.s. They were regulars in the bar. They have a history of arguing with each other. I thought perhaps they had both had a bit too much to drink. When the fight broke out I expected security to come and break it up. I wasn't aware of what was really happening until the Right Honourable Mr. Brace jumped on top of the Right Honourable Mr. McDonald and bit his throat out. I can still hardly believe it all. I saw blood pouring out of Mr. McDonald and I was sure he was dead. Then he got up. Then both men started attacking everyone in the bar. I barely escaped with my life.'

Mr Pollard began to sob to the camera.

'I am still in shock,' he blubbered.

The camera quickly cut away from Mr Pollard. The reporter stared briefly at the camera, looking as though he did not know what to say next. The presenter quickly snapped back into 'reporter mode' as scenes of Parliament Square were replayed on the television screen.

'It is not known how many people have been affected, but security services are speculating. There may have been a viral attack on the 13,000 pass holders who were present at yesterday's Parliament. Many of the pass holders who have not returned today are requested to report to their nearest police station, as they may have been infected with this virus. Most of the pass holders are still at large. A security cordon has been constructed around Westminster. The police are asking everyone to stay away, and to be vigilant.'

Isobel stared at Bubbles. Samn looked at Isobel sheepishly.

'13,000? 13,000 vampires roaming around London?' said Isobel.

'Yeah,' replied Samn ambiguously. 'That's too many vampires really, isn't it?'

Bubbles looked at Isobel and bit into one of her pink acrylic nails.

'Yeah, or thereabouts,' she replied. 'Don't be down hearted, Isobel. It was a success. Just, a little bit too much of a success.' Bubbles didn't seem to have been very affected by this turn of events.

'Just because one ritual has more bravado than another doesn't necessarily mean it isn't more effective than another. That knife in the square idea worked well. The other ritual on the heath, that was good too.' Bubbles added. 'I mean, it's not an exact science all of this. But since yesterday, the directors have had a change of heart about the volume. You might need to just quietly pull the vampires back a bit.'

'Oh, great.' Isobel watched as the man with the wet and dry vac packed up the canister full of glowing sludge. 'Just marvellous. So, where's he going with that shit? Off to make zombies?' exclaimed Isobel sarcastically.

'No, no-no,' said Bubbles. 'He'll use that for ghost distribution. That's no big deal honestly. Don't worry about that right now.'

'I am worried!' said Isobel. 'There's 13,000 vampires running around Parliament Square right now.'

Samn grabbed Isobel's arm.

'Sorry, Isobel,' he said, trying to console her. 'Not all of them are in the square. Some of them are out and about, probably back in their constituencies.'

Isobel shot him a fierce look. She pulled her arm away and started to pace up and down the living room.

Samn sat on the sofa. He and Bubbles shared a slightly sheepish look with each other.

Everyone went silent. Bubbles lit a cigarette and kicked one of her assistants as he walked past. Isobel walked up to Bubbles and put her hand out. Bubbles handed her a cigarette and offered her a light. Isobel folded her arms and glared at Samn.

'What are you going to do about this?' demanded Isobel.

Samn stared back silently and started processing his thoughts. Something did need to be done. He started.

'Now, if the werewolf *and* the vampire ritual worked then that's good. The fact that they had made too many vampires was just a problem and problems get solved,' he announced. 'So, we need to consider what resources we have and what we can do with them.'

Bubbles made to leave. 'I think I am just going to collect my canister of gloop and get rolling. It's nothing personal, kids, but this is your problem now and I have my own schedule to keep to.' One of the biohazard suited men made to walk towards the door with the canister.

'Oh no,' said Isobel. She grabbed the canister off the man. 'Oh no, you don't. That can stay right here until we figure how this is getting fixed. One or two werewolves, okay…I can live with that. Even a few vampires, that's par for the course around London. But we made an excess of vampires yesterday. There is no way I am letting that canister out of my sight until I know exactly what it is going to turn into.'

'They are just going to make a few ghosts. It's nothing major, I promise,' said Bubbles trying to play the subject down. 'Untwist your knickers, Mrs!'

Isobel glared at Samn.

'I will tell you what, Bubbles. *We* will look after this until his vampire issue gets sorted out. Tell whoever you need to tell that we wouldn't let you have the canister. And if anyone has a problem about that fact, just send them to me if they want to discuss the matter.'

Bubbles sighed and blew a raspberry at them.

'This wasn't cool, Samn.'

Isobel walked Bubbles to the door and opened it forcefully.

'Goodbye Bubbles, it's been lovely meeting you. Now you should go. Cheerio.'

A disgruntled Bubbles stomped out of the door, followed by her four crewmembers.

'As you wish,' said Bubbles. Isobel and Samn watched as she appeared beside the limousine downstairs. Bubbles looked up and gave them both the finger. She got into the limousine with her crew. It pulled away from the curb.

Isobel and Samn rushed back into the bedroom. They re-watched the scenes from Parliament on the news. Isobel retrieved the canister and set it down beside the bed. She stared long and hard at it.

'Let's stick that in the cupboard for now, until we decide what the hell to do with it. Its time to feed the cats,' she said pragmatically.

'Yeah and Brian,' said Samn, as an afterthought.

Brian hopped up on the bed and snuffled something into Samn's ear. He then snuffled in his ear a second time with a sharp sniff and walked towards the front door. He began scratching the door to get out.

'What's going on?' said Isobel.

'We have to let Brian out. He said if we let him out he can go find us some advice.'

'From who?' queried Isobel.

'At this juncture, does it matter who? I mean have you got a solution right now? I bloody don't!' Samn sounded exasperated.

'Well, no, but I thought Brian was just a watcher,' she replied.

'He is a watcher, but he's also my pal. If he says he can get us some advice, it can't hurt to try. Let him out,' said Samn.

Isobel opened the door and Sam darted out of the door. He swiftly swept past one of the neighbours as they were coming in through the entry door.

'How will he get out when he gets downstairs?' asked Isobel.

The downstairs door buzzed. Isobel went to the intercom phone and listened to the receiver. She heard a single bark. She buzzed the downstairs door.

'That made no sense whatsoever, but I guess he's out,' said Isobel. Her face was full of disbelief.

'Just leave him to it,' said Samn. 'And yeah, he is definitely a watcher. In fact, he recounted that he was quite pissed off that he wasn't allowed to watch us last night.'

'Not funny and not happening' said Isobel gruffly.

Isobel went through to the kitchen and began to feed the kittens. They seemed completely oblivious to everything except their cat bowls. Absent-minded, Isobel put a bowl of food out for Brian. The kittens began to sniff at it, but quickly returned to their interests to their brown, gravy-flavoured meat. She made two cups of coffee and found a clean ashtray. Then, returning from the kitchen she sat down on the bed beside Samn. They each lit up a cigarette. Isobel handed Samn a cup of coffee.

Isobel stared at the carnage on the TV screen. She watched as armed response teams fired at marauding, suited and booted vampires. In turn, the vampires grabbed the nearest bystanders and graphically bit out their throats. Helicopters circled above the scene on the TV. She looked out of the window at the sunny sky as a helicopter passed over her building. The helicopters on the screen were firing into crowds. Tourists, the press, businessmen and police alike darted chaotically around in front of the camera. They seemed to be marauding lawlessly at the square, looking for the next bystander to attack.

'13,000 vampires,' said Isobel with a lilt of exasperation. 'There's 13,000 vampires in town and some of them haven't even shown up for work today. This is just great. I thought vampires only came out at night?'

'Yeah. Well that's mostly true, about the night thing,' replied Samn. If they don't want to get caught, normally they do wait until it's dark out. But in an overstock vampire situation, it's more of a problem because they are in competition. That makes them a bit of a loose cannon. Then this happens,' replied Samn. He pointed to the TV screen. His voice sounded very matter of fact and disaffected by the current events.

'Marvellous,' said Isobel bluntly. 'So, how long will it be before *we* turn into vampires?'

'Oh, Brian will be back before any of that nonsense. Don't worry about that,' countered Samn dismissively. 'Besides, these flats are vampire apocalypse proof. Look at all those gate doors you have. They are brilliant.'

Isobel decided to fire several questions towards Samn. These came in rapid succession.

'How long is Brian going to be gone? Do you think he will be able to help? Where do you think he went?' she said.

'Listen, I can only guess. But he may have gone up the heath to speak to the werewolves or he may have popped back down to Soho to the portal, but that's just a guess. If he left, he left to try and get us some information. Even if I had asked him where he was going, he wouldn't have told me. He's always been like that, has Brian. He'd say he was going left, then go right.'

Isobel and Samn carried on watching the updates of chaos on the news and sipped coffee.

After a few hours, the buzzer went again. Isobel jumped up.

'It must be Brian!' she said excitedly. 'Although I don't know how he used the intercom.'

'He's a clever dog,' replied Samn.

She buzzed Brian through the second door. He meandered through the front door, followed by a second dog. They both went straight to his dog bowl.

Samn and Isobel stood tentatively over Brian. They were both waiting for the latest information from him. Brian unselfishly shared his food with the second dog. They both lapped up water from an adjacent dish. Brian walked slowly through to the living room. He was followed by the mystery canine. Samn stood in front of him. Brian extended a paw, trying to pull Samn down to his level.

Samn knelt beside Brian, who again snuffled something in Brian's ear.

Samn took a long look at Brian and screwed up his face a little.

'Brian says: That's Patricia. The other dog. She's on a different job.'

'I see,' said Isobel.

'He says, what?' Samn stared at Brian in disbelief. 'He says our services are required at Westminster.'

'How is that a solution?' demanded Isobel. 'We are going to end up as vampires if we do that.'

Samn looked at Brian squarely. 'Who said that? Patricia?'

Brian woofed once.

'Oh, for fucks sake Brian!' Samn stood up. 'Brian just intimated to me that Patricia is nothing to do this. He says he just brought her back here for a shag. For fuck's sake Brian, we have a mild crisis going on here!'

Brian woofed again.

'I am not becoming a vampire!' blasted Isobel. 'And we are definitely not going to Parliament!'

'We have to,' replied Samn. 'They want that canister. They've told Brian we are just to get the tube down to as close to Parliament as we can get.'

'Who are they?' said Isobel.

'My bosses,' Samn answered.

'If they want that canister so badly, why don't they just come and get it?' said Isobel.

'We don't want them to do that. Last time I

saw them they brought the building down. There were flames, burning books, riots, break dancing - all that. You don't want them here, I promise you.'

'We have that now anyway, tell Brian to go tell them they are going to have to come and get it if they want it. And tell him to take his little hussy with back to wherever he found her as well.'

Samn put his hands over Patricia's ears.

'Patricia will be hurt by that comment, shh!' said Samn. 'Don't fuck it up for Brian, he's my mate!'

'Come on, Isobel. Let's just get the bus back down to Westminster and see what they want. They can probably undo the vampires. If we give them the canister maybe they will do something like that.'

Isobel paced up and down the living room again.

'You know, I would greatly appreciate a few better answers before I agree to anything. I have been a pretty good sport about all of this up until now. When we made those werewolves, I didn't stay mad for long, did I? I was good about that. And when you told me we were turning a few parliamentarians into vampires; I admit, I thought, 'Good!' But now, we've got a canister of green goo and you want me to turn it over to people who are not competent enough to stop the centre of London from being overrun by vicious bloodsuckers. I just think it's time you explained the purpose of all this carnage if I am going to offer a continuance of my help.'

Samn looked patiently at Isobel. He gulped back the rest of his coffee.

'I suppose you do deserve and explanation. And yes, this was all my idea. I'll try to explain and hope you will understand. That's the best I can do. Every time I come up with a new idea that might be of interest to my directors, it's a bit like putting in for a planning application. It's like drawing up a kind of business plan. You project how you expect the plan will play out. Then after reading it, my bosses will give it a 'yay' or 'nay'.

'And *who are* your bosses, exactly?' petitioned Isobel.

'Who are *your* bosses? We have the same bosses. I just know them a little bit better than you do. I occasionally go drinking with them. They liked my last idea. Now they just want a chat. Maybe, we *should* go see them. They can help and perhaps explain things better to you than I can right now. Wouldn't that help?'

Isobel got up and walked through to the living room. She sat down at her desk and put her head on the keyboard, face down. One of the kittens jumped onto the desk and started to purr at her.

'I don't know what to do,' said Isobel, shaking her head from side-to-side over the keyboard.

The telephone rang. Isobel looked at it. A flat voice began speaking on the other end of the line.

'Hello? This is bubbles pizza may I take your order please?' said the voice in monotone succession.

'What? You called me!' said Isobel. 'I don't want any pizza!'

Isobel heard Bubbles as she grabbed the receiver at the other end of the line.

'Give me that phone, halfwit!' barked Bubbles. Her voice then softened to a one of charm.

'Halloo? Is that Isobel? I'm sorry. You just can't get the right staff these days,' sighed Bubbles. 'Listen you have got to take that canister to the directors. They want it.'

Isobel sighed.

'Even if I wanted to, which I don't, how am I going to get anything down past a huge police cordon and thousands of vampires?'

'We'll send a car for you. It will be fine. I promise! Please do this Isobel. If you do this, we can fix everything.'

Isobel huffed down the receiver. 'Oh God, alright! Ok, okay. At this point I just haven't got the energy to fight any more. Let's just give them what they want and then to hell with it all.'

Brian mouthed something to Samn. Samn turned to Isobel.

'Brian was a wondering if you could order him another pizza.'

'Shut up Brian!' reeled Isobel. 'No more pizza, whoredog! You just want us to get lost so you can shag Patricia!'

Chapter 11 Ghost Maker

Isobel walked into the bathroom and looked at Samn. He stared intently in the mirror as he shaved the stubble off of his chin.

'Are we bringing Brian with us?' she queried.

'We can if you want to, but we don't need to. We don't need a watcher where we are going. It's one less thing to think about as well. We should let him stay here with Patricia,' he replied. Samn shook out his razor in the cold soapy water of the sink.

'If I am going to meet your friends, what am I going to wear?' Isobel looked at him in the mirror, but Samn didn't meet her eyes. He carried on shaving.

'It doesn't matter what you wear, really. But it would be best if you wore something semi-formal. It's more respectful. Just make it look like you tried to look presentable for them. That will be enough. In honesty, you could show up there just dressed as yourself in daywear and they wouldn't bat an eyelid. They don't see us in the same way others do. They live on a different plane. They read living creatures a thousand diverse ways. It would take a long time to explain to you in a tangible way how they see people and things.'

'Okay, if you say so. I just needed a little reassurance that I wasn't going to make a bad impression. I feel like I am going to meet your parents for lunch for the first time. This is a bit weird for me. I am trying to coordinate an outfit that is nice enough to meet new people coupled with also being casual enough to be comfortable if we need to fight vampires. It's a difficult prospect. This level of fashion multitasking is something I am finding complicated. I still have images darting around my mind of hacking our way through vampire tourists and the security forces. And, what if I get bitten by a vampire? Even in a nice little black dress and heels, I am going to look a mess.'

Samn stopped shaving and looked at her.

'Well they are sending a car. And if these two have called a meeting, it's unlikely they are going to want to fraternise with us whilst we are covered in blood, growling and trying to rip everyone's throat out. I doubt they will let that happen. Isobel, you worry too much.'

Isobel stared back at him. She admired his sense of calm amidst the chaos.

'I guess so,' answered Isobel softly. 'I am feeling a bit bad about all of this. What if they are angry at me about everything? I mean, if I hadn't returned to the tree. If I hadn't consented to bring you here, then none of this would have happened. I feel responsible for this mess.'

'Well, you are and you aren't. Everyone makes choices and then lives with them. But look at how things were before. Ask yourself, were they worse, or better?'

'Worse,' stated Isobel.

'So, what choice did you really have?' said Samn. He wiped the last of the shaving foam from his face, then grabbed Isobel around her waist. He kissed her. 'It's all swings and roundabouts. It's all physics. You get some of the new things you want, but you give up other things that you already had. If you want life to get better, you must sacrifice your fear of change. I think that that, *is a good thing*. If you want to win, you have to play. You must step off the precipice. Don't waste your time analysing all the moves you made on your chess board. Just be proud of the fact that you had the audacity to play. I know my compatriots. And I know they will respect you just because you forced a change.'

Isobel thought for a moment about what he just said. It made her head swim a little.

'I'll get dressed.' she added, and walked through to the bedroom.

~

Samn and Isobel were now dressed and ready to go. They sat quietly on the sofa, waiting. The intercom system buzzed. Samn walked through to the hallway and answered the entry phone.

'That's the car Isobel. It's downstairs. Bring the canister.'

Isobel was now dressed in a knee-length brown lace-patterned dress and candy pink high heels.

'You look nice,' said Samn comfortingly.

'I still don't know where we are going, apart from dropping off this canister to make some sort of ghost apocalypse. I can't say I am all that excited,' grumbled Isobel.

Samn spied Isobel as she looked around the flat before they left. She seemed to be giving the room a worried look.

'We *are* coming back, you know,' said Samn. 'There's no need to act all ominous about leaving. We'll be back in no time, I promise.'

Isobel fluttered her eyelashes a couple of times involuntarily.

'That's good to know,' she said, half smiling.

Samn took her hand. They locked the door and headed

downstairs to the waiting car.

'Nice,' said Sam.

A driver was waiting for them. He was standing beside the back door of the vehicle. The door was open.

'This is a beautiful car,' said Isobel. They both got in. The car sped off.

Samn looked around inside the car.

'Hey, this an armoured car! That should make you feel safer, Isobel. Look, there are muzzle-sized holes in the glass. I think they are so you can fire a gun out of them. That's so cool! Hey, driver. What kind of car is this?' hollered Samn to the driver through the partition.

The man pressed an intercom button.

'This is a 1928 Cadillac V-8 Town Sedan. It used to belong to Al Capone. We made a few modifications to it. It is still indeed, an armoured car. And you are right about the glass. That's exactly what it was used for.'

'That's amazing. Thank you, driver,' replied Samn. He turned to squeeze Isobel's hand.

'Does that make you feel a bit better?' said Samn to Isobel. 'The directors clearly want us to get there safely, or they wouldn't have sent this car for us.'

Isobel looked out of the window.

'This isn't the way to Westminster,' she replied, 'This is the way to East London.'

'Are you sure?' said Samn.

'I'm positive,' she replied. 'Do your friends *ever* do anything they say they are going to do?'

'Sometimes, but I have learned not to question what they do too much. There's usually some sort of reason. Sometimes there's no reason. In fact, I have noticed that they tend to live by their whims. I think they do it because it helps break up the monotony of time for them, a bit.'

Soon the car journey was at an end. The sedan pulled up at a huge, imposing, municipal- looking white building. In the foreground, a massive circular fountain shot jets of water a hundred feet into the air. The driver stopped the car in front of the high-columned entrance and opened the door the let them out.

Samn and Isobel got out. They both looked at their surroundings.

Isobel looked wryly at Samn.

'This is Walthamstow Town Hall!'

'Is it?' asked Samn.

'Yeah, these are the council offices. I don't know what we are doing here,' remarked Isobel.

'I genuinely thought we were going to Westminster,' Samn countered. 'Maybe it's a bit too much of a mess down there. Might be just as well. I am sure that the directors have their reasons. I'll carry the canister. Let's go in.'

A studious looking secretary greeted them at the door. She was wearing a low-cut 1950's era dress and black-rimmed spectacles. Her hair was immaculately styled.

'If you both would come this way please. I will show you to your appointment,' said the studious-looking secretary.

The secretary walked beside Isobel and Samn through the vast and ornate wood-panelled halls of the building. The halls were long and seemed endless. The three past several frosted glass doors. The secretary stopped outside a door marked '123'.

'You can go in now,' said the secretary. She turned and left.

Samn twisted the door handle and politely ushered

Isobel in first. Samn put the canister down beside the door.

They found themselves inside a massive room. There was a beautiful fresco of a forest scene painted on the ceiling. On each wall were depictions of tall gilded, art nouveau style angels, each one bearing a different type of sword.

In the middle of the room was a simple brown 1940's antique desk. A massive devil-like creature was standing behind it, his face full of concentration as he looked at the woman below him.

Samn recognised the beautiful woman. She was busily deep-throating the black creature's enormous, grizzled cock. Samn cleared his throat and rapped on the inside of the door a couple of times, trying to gain their attention.

'Ahem,' said Samn.

The devil creature turned to face Samn and Isobel. The woman peered coyly over the desk.

'Oh!' she said leaping up from behind the desk. 'Do excuse me I was just finishing my breakfast. I do apologise. I just can't resist him sometimes. He's such a beast! … Boy, I had better not say *that* out loud. Someone might take that completely the wrong way. *That's happened.*'

The woman walked over to Samn. She swept her green leather-gloved hand along his face softly. She then extended her hand out to Isobel. Isobel shook her hand.

'Hi Samn. How's tricks? I take it this is Isobel. Is-obel,' replied the woman.

'Yes,' said Samn obligingly.

'Hi Isobel, it's lovely to meet you in the flesh. You can call me Giselle if you like. But what's in a name? Call me whatever you like, just don't call me Allan. Everyone's been calling me that lately and I totally hate that name.' Giselle showed off her figure. 'I mean, do I look like an 'Allan'? That sounds like an area manager for a carpet chain. Totally insulting!' She showed them to the desk. She pointed at the devil creature.

'That's Lou.'

Lou lifted a hand. He casually waved a "Hi". He then stretched and yawned.

'Do sit down,' said Giselle.

Samn and Isobel looked around at the room. There were no chairs to sit on.

After a moment Giselle realised the same thing.

'Oh, silly me. Hang on a minute,' she added. She sounded slightly flustered. 'I do forget sometimes.'

Giselle extended her hand and pointed at two spaces in the room. Two chesterfield-style, button-backed leather chairs appeared. Isobel and Samn sat down, facing the desk.

Lou perched on the desk in a relaxed stance whilst rearranging his beautifully cut tweed suit.

'Did you bring the canister?' asked Giselle efficiently.

'Oh yes, it's by the door,' replied Samn. 'There was reluctance to bring the canister, after yesterday's debacle,' he added. 'But we decided it was better to stick to the plan.'

Lou raised an eyebrow at Samn.

'How unusual,' said Lou.

Isobel puffed herself up a little bit. She decided to address this curious looking pair with a degree of fearlessness.

'It's nice to meet you both. I have heard a lot about you. So please, don't get me wrong when I say I am slightly perturbed about bringing the canister along to this meeting. So far, I have been going along with this entire plan, hoping that my involvement would be in some way beneficial to the situation. But I have still yet to see any positive results, despite the reassurances that there would be some. As far as I can see it, this scheme has only transgressed into something worse.'

Giselle laughed. 'No, not at all! We had a few teething problems yes, that's true. But overall, we are right on target. And your life has improved, has it not?'

Isobel looked at the couple with a side glance.

'Who are you?'

'Well, I am Giselle and this is my husband Lou,' she reiterated.

'Are you two devils?' said Isobel in disbelief.

'Well obviously Lou is. But I'm not! she said with a laugh in her voice. 'Guess again.'

Isobel stared at them both in total disbelief.

'You are saying that Lou is a devil and you are… not a devil? I don't believe it.'

'None other than,' said Lou. 'As far as guessing who Giselle is, think of the last person on earth that you would expect to see, here.'

'Well, I did make you all in my image,' said

Giselle. 'Call it vanity, but I felt like keeping a good body back for myself today. I mean I appreciate beautiful things as much as the next person. I had to bitch slap that Da Vinci when he got to my realm after he worked out my golden ratio. That was so annoying. I told him, if he published that, that it wouldn't be long before people started rebelling against it. Now look at everybody. It's a bloody mess out there. He should have kept that shit to himself.'

Isobel glanced back and forth at Giselle and Lou with a furtive glance.

'I thought that you two didn't get along…' said Isobel.

'Oh, that was a long, long time ago,' sighed Giselle. She waved her hands dismissively. 'We had a little marital dispute. Then things got out of hand.'

Lou put his hand out to touch Giselle's.

'I am so sorry honey,' he said. He frowned, consoling her.

Giselle looked up at Lou and put her hand over his.

'What sort of dispute?' said Isobel boldly.

'Brave little thing isn't she, Samn? You tell her all this privileged information and yet she's still digging for more,' said Giselle with a laugh. 'I like the spirit of that.'

Giselle stared at Isobel for a long, hard moment with one eye closed. She sat down at the desk and folded her hands in front of her chin. She seemed to be reading into Isobel's mind. She then looked over towards Samn. She gave him a nod. Samn nodded back.

'I think I *will* tell you. Let's just say, a long time ago Lou and I got into a heated discussion about the creation of humanity. I enjoy creating things. I am an artist. At the time, I was very happy with the humans and the way that they were gradually progressing. But Lou, ever the one to rely on his charts and mathematical theories, had a different view. He claimed via his projections that ultimately 95% of the human population would turn out to be a bunch of assholes. I took exception to this statement at the time. I took it as a personal criticism about one of my new art pieces. But I shouldn't have. When I gave them free will and the ability to make their own choices, I felt certain that everything would work out fine. During that dispute, Lou and I had to go our separate ways. Then we went through a sustained period of trying to prove the other one wrong. But recently, both of our views converged.'

Lou folded his hands and crossed his legs. He listened to Giselle intently.

'Those were some dark times. I missed you

terribly. I hate it when we fight, pussycat,' Lou added.

'As do I, darling,' replied Giselle softly. She reached out to caress his arm.

Giselle clapped her hands together.

'So! As time passed, we watched. We watched the humans run the course of their evolution. Loathing as I am to admit it in this instance, Lou was correct. He was correct for the main part, anyway. Giving the humans so much free will *did* turn most people into assholes, as he predicted. There have been so many instances over the past several hundred thousand years that I have watched the murder, the carnage, the bloodletting, the animal disrespect, the human sacrifice, the wars, the serial killers… I watched all of it. Sometimes I was so horrified from watching that I had to escape from for weeks at a time. It was so hideous I couldn't even bear to keep an eye on this universe, let alone the Earth. I felt very betrayed by the humans. I was thankful when Brian offered to help watch things for me. I was thankful for all the watchers that tendered their services. They were the only ones with enough true empathy to protect me from the horror. The humans, now proving to be a gargantuan portion of assholes, had managed to turn all the extremely complex and challenging work I had created in my studio into bullshit. It was like they turned my planet into a huge, decadent, arseholic party zone. I felt like they had thrown a shitty party in my house without my permission. They pissed in my fishpond, burned down my shed and then had a fight in the living room. After that, for a long while I didn't like the humans. I still loved you all, but not enough to let you to enact any further destruction to me personally. No parent likes to watch their children fighting. But the real 'fuck you all' came from me when you started killing my pets. I felt a lot of anger and discord about it. There were times when I found myself laughing when every volcano and earthquake wiped another swathe of those selfish human cunts out. Tell me, who could watch all that for so many thousands of years and still retain an unbiased view of the human race? Watching the blinkered diminished capacity of death dealing became so repetitive it felt like listening to a broken record. Lou's mathematical calculations were right. They *were* almost entirely assholes. Then Samn came along with this great idea about bringing back the old monsters. We suggested to Samn that England would be the perfect starting place.'

'Why England?' said Isobel curiously, 'and why Samn?'

Lou strode across the room and stood beside Samn. He spoke.

'Samn is our top boy. Well actually he is Anubis's kid. But that's not what I mean. Samn is the founder of the "Society for the Ethical Treatment of Deities." He was the first one to campaign for our rights. He was the first one to ask everyone to cut us some slack. We like that about him. He's a keeper, that

Samn. He could see we were struggling. He had our back.'

Giselle intervened.

'We chose England, because they are not afraid of being the first place for new things to happen,' said Giselle reflectively. 'They have been consistent about this. And they are a tremendous bunch of copers. Many British people have a certain type of mindset that affects the rest of the world in a very surreptitious way. It's not the only district that does that. But it's one of the few. We thought this would be as good a springboard as any, for the implementation of our plan. That, plus Lou. He is skilled at dark, atmospheric design on your end of existence. I find that endearing about him. It's been a much better working relationship since we got back together. He's such a good bunny. He comes up with such good inventions and refreshingly dark concepts. His inventive ideas really break up the monotony for me sometimes. I love that about him.'

'Enemies,' said Lou calmly. 'humans, by their very nature need enemies. The animal part of them needs to fight and take territory. It comes naturally to them, even when they aren't observing that truth about themselves. But lately, they have settled into something quite imbalanced. Many times, in the past, I would receive word that Giselle was once again trying to talk the humans out of the fighting and the destruction. She'd grab a random human by the scruff of the neck and say "Here, write this down and show it to people." But, every single time she did that, her words would get twisted round. It was a thankless task. They would use what she said to gain more money, power, sex, territory or whatever they thought they needed to be happy. I take no issue with that personally, but that is mostly because I am here to create the contrast. I admit, it made me exasperated watching her try to get through to various humans, only to watch Giselle's ardour and trust become dissipated so cruelly by some new twat. All that religious shit that was written down in the past several thousand years, is now miserably out of date. It's all been lost in translation for centuries, sometimes longer. It's nothing to do with anything now. It's all such bullshit.'

'Fucking waste of time,' sighed Giselle. 'You try to talk to people reasonably, but giving out the slightest bit of helpful information seems to turn some individuals into self-appointed pricks. I worked my ass off putting so many beautiful creatures and landscapes on the earth, then I threw one curve ball in the form of humans. Before you knew it, they fucked up everything in sight and there was no turning back from it. It's been a fucking waste of time, that. Do you know how long it takes just to design a lizard? I did thousands of those little buggers. Did *anyone* appreciate any of that? No! You know, I haven't got a bank account or a pen either. I resent all these religions with a bank account, lying, claiming they are collecting money for me. When I see that, I run a fucking mile. I resent anyone with a pen, forging my name on laws that tell people what to do, then saying it's ok because "I said so." Nothing is achieved by sitting around idle in a religious institution blaring out boring hymns and prayers to me. Why can't those fuckers divide their time by preserving my earth? I'd appreciate that a great deal more. And the pressure, the pressure I feel. Everyone on this planet thinks when they die they will be standing at my right shoulder. How many shoulders do they think I have? You humans, you act like you own me the way a spoiled child thinks they own their Mum. I had a life, long before any of you were born. I have family and friends that know me far better than any of you ever will. None of you will ever be allowed to get that close to me. You're all just acquaintances now. That's also the reason why my partner Lou and I are so tight again.'

Isobel stood up and walked towards the windows. She stared outside.

'Lou is my best friend. If you want some advice on how to best to act sane, watch the animals. They destroy nothing and leave no mess. You will learn more about how to be a useful member of this planet by watching a snail, or an insect, or a snake, for that matter. You'll never learn it from a book, because anything written by a human is always flawed. Animals don't need monsters. It's just you lot that do. The way I feel right now, the animals are sane, but the jury is out on the humans. I wish I had just kept the space for them. I am also sad that all the valuable consciousness that I distributed to the humans got wasted. I feel like I have been rolled in a ditch like a bum. The humans fleeced me. I am not saying I hate all of you, I am just saying I am relieved when some of you leave the planet. Another thing you don't know, is that that free will doesn't end when you die. You go where you want to. But if you were a shit bomb to other people or other creatures they all have just as much right to tick the box that keeps you out of their realm on my side of existence. It's pretty fucking lonely for some people over there, that's all I can say.'

Giselle stood up and yawned loudly.

'The only humans left that I will still try to help, are some of the old ladies down towards the West Indies. They still seem to be trying to do the right thing, even when nobody is looking,' Giselle sighed. 'I suppose there's a lot of people I put here on the earth that have proved me wrong. Maybe that's what keeps this project going. I valued the opinion of the alternative sexuality people, the out-of-the-box thinkers, the atheists and everyone else in that vein. I put them there, because I wanted them there. It's no human's business to persecute the decisions I make. I have my reasons. And thanks to Samn's encouragement, I also have the right to not need to quantify any of it. The humans that are stuck in one, unchanging polarity of view, well, I mostly need a break from them for a good long minute. They shouldn't blame me for choosing to abandon them. I woke them up, and they chose to go back to sleep, so it's not my fault. The monotony of watching them making the same mistakes repeatedly has led me to believe that a new, more practical solution is required to sort out this mess.'

Lou put his hand on Giselle's shoulder. He continued for her.

'So, this is how we came to decide that if the humans wouldn't agree to stop fighting with each other, we should give them more challenging entities to fight with. We don't really want to interfere that much, but we *are* your landlords. And you *are* fucking our project up. At least now, the humans can share a common enemy.'

Isobel shifted in her seat and listened. Giselle continued.

'We now feel there's no need now for you humans to make monsters of each other. Leave the monster-making to us. When you look at the overall landscape of the situation, we both feel we have done the right thing. Just because it doesn't look like it on paper doesn't mean it won't have the desired corrective qualities in the long run. I mean, who has time for war if they are being stalked by werewolves and devoured by vampires? It's a hell of a distraction! You have to admit!'

Lou stroked her hair.

'Don't get yourself upset, dear.' He rolled his eyes as he looked at Isobel.

'She can have such a terrible temper sometimes. It can be very hard to calm her down.'

'May I smoke?' said Isobel.

'Yes of course you may,' replied Lou.

Isobel lit a cigarette. Samn followed her lead. The secretary entered the room and put a standing ashtray between the two chairs, then left.

'You know,' said Isobel. 'Thirteen thousand vampires marauding around London seems a harsh a solution.'

'Oh, I agree,' said Giselle emphatically. Lou nodded in unison. 'But we can remedy that with your offerings from last night. We like sex. After all, we invented sex. We like sex where everyone agrees with the idea, and is having fun. That's what *we* do. We gave the matter a lot of thought. I think we just need to pull the vampires back a bit and redirect the contents of that canister towards something different. Originally, the plan with the canister was to deposit quantities of the glowing goo in various locations around London, just to brighten the place up with a few ghosts, wraiths and spectres. You know, just to distract people. Initially we saw it as a bit of fun, to freak people out a bit, on top of the werewolves and vampires. But Lou came up with another idea. It's an improvement on the first plan. He's good like that.'

Lou clasped his hands together.

'Yes, I realised that the sludge in the canister would be just as effective for demonic possessions as it would be for providing hauntings. All we needed to do after that was find some young, fit candidates that could tackle the vampire problem. We needed some very driven people who wouldn't be intimidated by all those wild, rabid MPs creeping around the capital right now.'

'And we found a solution,' interjected Giselle. 'Sex workers.'

'We are going to distribute the ectoplasm in brothels, table dancing bars, dungeons and sex worker's flats. We think these adult industry workers will make fine vampire hunters once they have been possessed by the slime. I think this will get this little faux pas cleared up quickly, without too much mess,' said Lou.

Samn stared at them both in shock. Isobel then stared at Samn.

'That… could… work, I guess,' said Samn.

'There's only one way to find out!' said Giselle. 'Besides, it will liven things up a bit. I like a bit of action.'

Giselle pressed the button on an intercom.

'Marsha, do you think you could bring a television in here for me please?' she said politely.

After a few moments the secretary returned, wheeling a television into the room. She then lifted the canister and exited the room quietly.

'There it goes!' said Lou.

He hopped up off the desk. With his powerful animal-like legs, he stomped over to the television set. He switched on the news. More scenes of carnage flashed across the television screen. It appeared that the police had moved in. They were wielding a water cannon at the crowds. A clip of the newly-vampired Prime Minister attacking the armed forces flashed across the screen.

'Oh dear,' said Giselle. 'Oh dear,' she said, stifling a giggle.

'Well, I could have guessed that would happen,' said Isobel. 'All Prime Ministers are self-serving vampires. This time, it's just being done in public.'

'True, but let's not watch any more of this car crash TV,' said Giselle intently. 'There's no reason why we can't skip forward to tomorrow.'

Giselle walked up to the T.V. screen. With a sweeping movement from her hand, flicked the screen from left to right.

'Now, it's tomorrow,' she said with a smile.

Isobel, Samn and Lou viewed the screen with interest. Lou turned up the sound so they could hear the report.

A solemn-voiced news presenter stood in Parliament square. Behind him were scenes of wildly possessed looking sex workers. They were driving stakes through many of the suited and booted parliamentary vampires.'

'Well, that's different,' said Isobel, still smoking.

The presenter began to give his report:

'In the wake of yesterday's carnage, there was an unusual turn of events. It is reported that a large number of sex workers have turned out in force to tackle the capital's new vampire problem. What has spurned this aspect of society into action is not known, but it's seems to be taking effect. Men and woman were seen armed with wooden stakes. We don't know how this situation transpired. There have been unconfirmed reports that the escorts were disgruntled over unpaid bills from some of the Parliamentary members. Many of the escorts have been here in Westminster, dealing with what is being treated as a massive infestation of vampires. Now, with most members of parliament now deceased, it is unknown how the country plans to continue. Many are just thankful that this dreadful, unusual siege is now over. George Browning, reporting live, from Westminster.'

'See?' said Giselle, 'That wasn't so bad! I think Bubbles sent some of her boys down to assist all the sex workers. I think she sent stakes, and full details of the Parliamentarians unpaid accounts with the sex workers. I guess that was enough to turn the corner for the ensuing rage. Good, no?'

Giselle opened her desk and produced an ornate bottle of liquid. She presented it to Samn.

'In fact, let's just stay at "tomorrow" now. I think yesterday is best left alone. You've both seen what has happened. None of this is an exact science, but at least we have cleared a path for you. All you need to do, is nip down to parliament and sprinkle this liquid around the square. Just beware of surprise vampires. I am pretty sure you can outrun them. They are weak in the daytime. Or if you really feel in danger, try and borrow a hooker for protection from somewhere. I hear they are still pretty pissed off. This liquid will help cull the extra vampires back. It's like ice cubes on the bollocks for them. Now, off with you two. I enjoyed our meeting, but the car is waiting!' said Giselle. 'Bye-bye Isobel, Bye-bye Samn.'

Samn and Isobel took the bottle and raised themselves out of their chair. Lou and Giselle stood up looking at them both expectantly. They waved politely and gave them both a cheesy smile.

'Have fun!' said Giselle sweetly, 'and Thank-you!'

The secretary opened the door. She stood patiently waiting, ready to walk them out.

Isobel looked down at the bottle.

'What does this do?' she said to Samn.

'They want us to sprinkle it around Parliament square. I am hoping it will neutralise most of the vampires.

But you never know with those two. I hope whatever is in this bottle, doesn't end up making everything worse.'

'Well, let's just do it and get it over with. Hopefully by then, we will both be off the hook for a while.'

Samn and Isobel got back into the sedan.

'Driver, take us to Westminster. Parliament Square please,' said Samn.

The car sped off towards the centre of Town. Isobel and Samn sat silently, watching the scenery race past the sedan window.

Samn turned to Isobel.

'Have you thought about what you will do with old Sam after this?'

'Yes,' she replied.

'What are you going to do, then?' he probed.

'Well, if you were shagging the son of Anubis, would you take your ex back?' she smiled. 'No... I wouldn't either,' she said with a mischievous giggle. 'Samn, I want to thank you for finding me. What I know now means a great deal to me. Before I met you, I thought my heart was dead. And now it's not. I would have to be insane to let that go. I will adjust to this alternative reality provided you stay in it. Whatever you are Samn, is right for me. I'm done with the past. Old Sam can just paddle his own canoe. Now let's get this task sorted and see if it balances things out.'

Isobel turned to address the driver. She shouted through the partition.

'Driver, keep the engine running when we get there. 'Because after this, I want to go home. I'm hungry and I want to fuck.'

'Yes, Ma'am,' said the driver.

The sedan barrelled towards town.

THE END

Printed in Great Britain
by Amazon